DAMAGED

DAMAGED

TAYE KNOX

Published by J Merrill Publishing, Inc.
A division of J Merrill One
434 Hillpine Drive
Columbus, OH 43207
www.JMerrill.pub

Library of Congress Control Number: 2026908080

Paperback ISBN: 978-1-961475-70-0
eBook ISBN: 978-1-961475-71-7

Printed in the United States of America
First Edition

10 9 8 7 6 5 4 3 2 1

J Merrill One™ and J Merrill Publishing™ are trademarks of J Merrill One.

Portions of the editorial and publishing workflow may have been enhanced using proprietary AI systems developed by J Merrill One.

TABLE OF CONTENTS

BETRAYAL HAS A SOUND

Sitting at the spot, we had just finished setting the trap niggas straight with some work, I yelled out, "Alright Money, I'm out this bitch!"

"Yo Stoney, where you headed?" Robert called back.

"I'm about to run over to Sky's crib right quick! She's about to bless a nigga!" I laughed.

Sky was this chick I met at school, real chill. We had linked up after running into each other at the mall a few weeks back.

She stayed close to the spot, so it was nothing to slide through.

"Aye, Stone, your dick gone fall off fuckin' with these birds!" Mookie joked from downstairs.

"She be huntin' a nigga down to get this work!" I shot back, stepping through the door.

I heard him talking as I was closing the door.

"One day one of them birds gone get yo' ass! Don't be surprised if one of 'em come up pregnant!"

I laughed at his dumb ass before slamming the door.

I walked a little down the path behind the spot. Something felt off.

I kept walking past an old hoopty, but I couldn't shake the feeling.

"Shit," I muttered beneath my breath.

My eyes shifted to the house a few doors down from the trap.

It was a little three-bedroom we bought to get off the radar—tired of always sitting at the trap.

Nobody knew we owned it. We liked having shit tucked away.

I looked to my left, the spot was empty.

The top niggas were supposed to be posted, but they weren't.

I stopped and glanced right.

That's when I saw a car creeping past the trap, going real slow.

I recognized it. It was a cop.

He flashed his badge a few weeks ago when he stopped a kid in the neighborhood.

Mistook him for a twenty-year-old who robbed a gas station.

The boy was just fifteen, headed home from school.

"What the fuck?" I mouthed.

Reaching into my pocket, I dialed Money.

Just as he picked up, I heard the takedown.

"GET YOUR HANDS UP! GET ON THE GROUND! DON'T MOVE OR I'LL TAKE YOUR HEAD CLEAN THE FUCK OFF!"

Voices boomed in sync as they busted through the archway.

Everyone leaping off the couch, hands held above their heads.

Commands rang out as the DEA crashed in—storming room to room, tearing through shit, ripping mattresses, smashing mirrors.

Bringing in K-9s.

One by one, they dragged out the crew.

I had ducked off into our hidden spot.

"Who is it?" Tiffany called out, panic in her voice.

"It's me, Tiff. I need to see what the fuck is going on next door."

She opened the door, and I took the stairs two at a time.

From the second floor, I pulled back the curtain.

Watched it all unfold.

The same car from earlier was now parked across the street. Instead of one person, now there were two people sitting inside.

My heart sank.

Betrayal's a bitch.

ACT I

ORIGINS & WOUNDS

1

BEFORE THE FALL

Growing up, we would hit the court with a few guys from the neighborhood, betting a hundred dollars a pop. We could afford to bet five a game without batting an eye, but we preferred to stay low.

Swish! The ball snapped the net.

"Damn, Money!" we hollered, fists covering our mouths.

He was about to take the ball out when a girl wearing a miniskirt strolled by, looking fine as hell with legs for days.

"One day, I'm going to find out who those legs belong to!" Mario muttered, biting his lip.

"Hell yeah! See if her ass got a friend!" Robert added.

"The game, nigga!" Mookie barked, drilling the ball into Robert's chest.

All of us watched the girl continue down the street until she disappeared.

After the game, I hooked up with my girl Sky for the rest of the night.

We had a routine back then. Drop Ant at junior high before we made it to the high school, before circling back to the trap. On graduation day, I took Ant home, dropped Robert and Mookie off at the trap spot before heading to our house.

We let Tiffany and her baby live there after seeing her several times wandering the streets pushing a stroller. We never served her, and we didn't hear about her getting served anywhere else, so the decision was easy.

She had fallen on hard times after leaving her son's father. She knew we used the house from time to time—mainly hanging out in the basement we had turned into our man cave. Sometimes she cooked dope for us when we didn't have time to do it ourselves, which kept money in her pockets.

I called Tiffany before leaving school, letting her know I'd be stopping by. I knocked twice before using the key. I didn't expect her to be there, so I was surprised when she rounded the corner.

"Hey, Tiff, this is my friend Sky," I said, introducing them.

"Hi, Ms. Tiffany," Sky smiled and waved.

Tiffany smiled, returning the wave, but cut her eyes.

I caught the attitude Tiffany threw at Sky, brushing it off. I guided her downstairs.

When we reached the bottom, I ran my fingers around the brim of her shorts. "You better have panties on," I whispered.

She giggled. Sky was a tease.

"Take that shit off," I growled.

"We can't do that with your sister home!" she giggled, teasing me but did it anyway.

Reaching inside the drawer, I grabbed a loose condom.

She protested, "You don't need that! I'm on birth control."

I continued rolling the condom. My number one rule—never fuck raw.

When we were done, we dressed quietly.

"Aye, go ahead and get in the car. I'll be there in a second," I said, tossing my head towards the garage. I needed to see what was up with ole' girl. I didn't care for the diss from earlier.

"Hey," Tiffany said, wiping her hands.

"What's up with that earlier?" I asked.

She shrugged. "I don't know what you're talking about."

"She didn't deserve your attitude, Tiff," I countered.

"Stoney, it's just that you can do so much better than her," she said.

I stepped into her personal space. Slightly irritated. "That shit doesn't matter. She's just somebody I'm kicking it with right now."

Out of nowhere, she pecked my lips.

"Aye, what the fuck, Tiff?" I stepped back.

"Why not, Stoney? You like her, but you don't like me?"

"Nah, it's just that you're like my sister," I said, shifting my eyes toward the garage. The last thing I needed was Sky walking in on whatever this was.

Her gaze dropped. "Well, I'm not your sister."

I ran my hand down my chin. Truth was, Tiffany was a bad bitch—I couldn't lie about that. She was stronger than most females her age. As bad as I wanted to return the kiss, I couldn't cross that line.

Softening my tone, "look, I gotta go. I need to get Sky home."

I released a hard breath and turned to leave. When I glanced back, Tiffany was just staring at me.

"It's about time," Robert snapped as I pulled up.

"Awe, here we go," I chuckled. "Nigga, get in!" Unlocking the doors.

"Where's Mook?"

"Grabbing something to smoke before we hit Faith's crib."

I filled him in on what happened earlier with Tiffany.

"Word?" His eyes bulging.

"Word," I said, checking my face in the rearview mirror.

"Why didn't you hit?"

"Nah, she's cool, but she's like a sister." Shaking my head. "Plus, I had Sky with me."

Mookie strolled toward the car with a blunt dangling from his lips. When he hopped in the back seat, he immediately started going in.

"Why the fuck you take so long, my nigga?" he barked.

We slapped hands. "Now sit yo' ass back!" I joked.

"Damn, Gee, why you do my nigga like that?" Robert teased.

We laughed as I drove toward Faith's house. Her family was uppity and didn't like people who didn't have money.

I rang the doorbell, and we put on our white boy persona.

"Hi, Mrs. Patterson. Is Faith home?" I grinned.

"Hi, Mario, Faith is in her room." "Hi, boys!" Mrs. Patterson chortled, speaking to Robert and Mookie. They smiled but didn't speak.

My Timberlands thudded loudly with each step I took up the spiraling staircase. Faith was biracial—her mother was white; her father was a stuck-up nigga who thought he was better than the average black man. He's the type we'd fuck up if we caught him slipping in the street.

Her mom knocked twice before opening her door. "Faith, your friends are here."

She leaped from her bed and rushed me at the door, hugging my neck tight.

"Wait until your moms is gone!" I whispered. She pecked my lips instead of responding.

Mookie pulled a joint from behind his ear.

"Yooo, you had that in front of her moms?"

"Yeah! So?"

I shook my head at his crazy ass. "Whatever," I chuckled.

"Her moms know what's up!" he said with a stupid smirk on his face.

After chilling for about an hour, things started dying down.

"Where's your homegirl?" Robert asked.

Faith took the joint from Mookie and took a pull. "She's working," she said, blowing a cloud of smoke.

"Don't tell me about Tracy—I don't wanna know!" Mookie slurred, roaring with laughter like he told a funny joke. I looked at his stupid ass with a "shut the fuck up" expression.

"Shut up, Mookie! She's on her way, as a matter of fact!" Giggling, she tossed a pillow at him, making us laugh.

A half hour later, Tracy walked in.

"Hey, y'all!" greeting everyone. She greeted Robert with a hug and mean-mugged Mookie.

I slightly looked over at him. He pulled her onto his lap as we continued talking and getting high.

A few minutes later, Mookie stood, holding Tracy's hand.

"We're going to step out on the balcony," he announced, telling me and Robert through code.

Faith remained on my lap, snuggled in my arms, while Robert continued scrolling through his phone.

"When are you coming to see me by yourself?" she whispered.

Robert raised his head slightly, turning to look back at me just long enough for me to notice.

I hesitated. "My brothers and I do everything together. Why is that a problem now?"

Her eyes hooded. "It's not a problem," she sighed.

I hooked her chin, urging her to look at me.

"I'll come by myself next week," I promised.

Her eyes lit up. She planted a soft kiss on my lips.

I lied, because I didn't like being in a white neighborhood at night. You never knew what kind of crazy shit would pop off.

We bounced when my phone buzzed.

"Yo!" I answered without checking the caller ID.

"Where have you been, Mario? I've been calling you for an hour," Sky barked. She was mad as hell.

I ran my hand down my face before sighing.

"Yo, look—I'm out with my peoples!"

"Is that the only reason you didn't call me back?" She yelled.

"Look, I'm not cut for this shit. Maybe we should just call it quits," I stated calmly.

She gasped. "No! I don't want to break up!"

"Fuck," I cursed. I was low-key tired of dealing with her shit. "Then chill the fuck out!"

The phone fell silent.

"Okay," she whispered.

I didn't wait for her to say anything else. I disconnected the call, giving her time to sit with that shit.

2

———

SISTER, NOT LOVER

When I first arrived at the juvenile detention facility, I made regular calls to check on Tiffany.

"What's up, Tiff?"

"Hey, Stoney, how are you holding up?" She sounded happy to hear from me.

"I'm holding. They're moving me this week to an adult facility. I turned eighteen in this bitch!" I groaned.

I could hear the smile in her voice.

"Happy birthday, Stoney!" she said cheerfully.

I'm not sure why, but I smiled from a true place.

"Yo, thanks, Tiff!"

We chatted up—neighborhood gossip to the word on the streets about the bust. We kept our conversations coded whenever we talked.

Then her tone shifted.

"Stoney, can I ask you a question?"

I sensed the uneasiness in her voice, giving me an uncomfortable feeling.

"Yeah, always."

I leaned on the cold, damp wall, anticipating her question. She cleared her throat.

"Why haven't you ever tried to talk to me?"

Caught off guard, I wasn't expecting her to ask that. I thought she was going to ask for a couple of bands or something to get by.

Now it was time for me to clear my throat.

"Look, Tiffany, we're very good friends—to the point, you're like a sister to me. That's something a nigga like me don't take lightly!"

I could hear her breathing change.

"Is it because I have Junior?"

"Tiffany, you having a kid is never a problem. I care a lot about you and Junior. You deserve someone who can give you everything you're looking for."

I changed the conversation.

"Are you straight? Do you need money, food, or anything?"

"No, I don't need anything. I appreciate y'all for looking out for us."

I ran down some important things I needed her to handle before time ran out. I also made sure she understood what to do if and when she heard from Robert or Mookie.

3

—————

LOYALTY UNDER FIRE

After the bust, Zander's phone buzzed. He snatched it from the nightstand.

"Yeah!" he barked.

"Aye yo, it's Buster! The spot just got raided an hour ago!"

Zander sat straight up. "What do you mean they got raided? What the hell happened? Get Barry Dawson on the phone! Pay him whatever he asks for. They need to be out tonight! Once they get out, have them meet me at the spot!" He hung up before Buster could respond.

Two hours later, Attorney Barry Dawson had successfully bailed out the crew.

Zander's phone buzzed again; this time he remained quiet. Dawson's voice came through the receiver.

"Your guys are out. It'll cost you big this time. First appearance in two months—you know how this goes. I don't need to explain the rest. See you in two months." With that, Dawson disconnected the call.

Back at the spot, the mood was tense.

"Look at your scary ass!" Loco taunted, clowning as if the raid was a joke. Loco laughed loudly. "What, that shit ain't fun for you no more?"

He was getting on my fucking nerves.

"Aye yo, shut the fuck up!" I snapped, my voice heated.

The door creaked open. Buster walked in, followed by Zander. His boots echoed like thunder.

"Anybody wanna tell me what the fuck happened tonight? How MY spot got raided!" he hissed.

They averted his gaze, not wanting to provoke another one of Zander's shooting sprees—a reaction he often had over minor grievances.

Mookie leaned back with a menacing glare, chewing on a toothpick like the calm before the storm. We were definitely on whatever time he was on, keeping heat on our hips at all times. I stood to my full height, tired of Zander's ranting and his attempts to intimidate us.

"Look, nobody knows what the fuck happened. The feds came from nowhere!" I brushed my hand down my chin, something I did when I was frustrated.

"What happened to those top niggas? They didn't sound the alarm! We were about to get hit, and they chose not to say shit?"

My eyes swept the room. Loco and Base refused to meet my gaze.

I knew they set this shit up. In my eyes, if a man avoided eye contact, he was weak. Untrustworthy.

The sudden boom in Zander's voice pulled me back.

"Come on, somebody knows something!" he mocked, scanning the room, calling niggas out one by one, choosing to ignore me.

"So, can't NOBODY tell me shit, huh?"

Zander roared, pulling his Glock from his waistband, pointing it at Loco.

"NOW can a nigga tell me something?"

Loco trembled violently, ready to crack.

My expression remained unfazed.

"On life, my nigga, I'll find out what the fuck happened."

Zander smirked.

I stepped forward, ice in my eyes. Neither one of us willing to back down.

Mookie tapped my chest.

"Yo Money, let's bounce, bruh!"

My eyes locked on Zander.

"Yeah, let's bounce!"

We eased out, burners evident. Reaching outside, we climbed into the parked Lexus.

Mookie blew a sigh. "Yooo, what was that shit about?"

"Nothing. I refuse to let that nigga think he controls me." I growled, peeling away from the curb.

When we reached the house, I texted Tiffany: *We're outside and we'll be up in a second.* She sent a single reply: *Okay.*

We entered through the back door, checking our surroundings. Your life was only worth the next come-up in this game.

Tiffany rounded from the kitchen, greeting us with hugs. Mookie read the room, abruptly walking into the kitchen for a glass of water.

"Tiff, have you seen or heard from Stoney?"

"You know, the day y'all got knocked, Stoney had just left y'all at the spot. That's when he noticed something happening outside. He came here running upstairs, seeing the hit," she whispered.

My eyes locked on hers.

"What's up, Tiff?" I asked sternly, letting her know I didn't have time for the bullshit. "You saying he saw the takedown and didn't say nothing?"

"He tried calling you, but it happened so fast." She paused before she remembered one last thing. "He gave me a key to hold until he came home or until I saw one of y'all," she said.

"What does the key belong to?" Mookie asked.

She shrugged. "I don't know, but I still have it if you want to see it. I know you're really tight and—" Looking at me, her voice trailed.

"Let us see the key," Mookie said, softer than I had been earlier.

She went upstairs, returning with a Morehouse keychain; a single key dangled. Mookie accepted it, holding her hand a bit longer than necessary.

"Thank you, baby," he said, examining the key.

"Yo, remember this key?" Mookie whispered.

I grabbed the key, searching for any clue it might hold. Then it hit me —it belonged to a storage unit we used when Ant was at Morehouse. We used the storage to stash our money there in case we got hit. We initially stashed the money as well as a few bricks for when we were ready to step out on our own, totaling thirty million dollars in work and cash.

"Tiff, look, I apologize. I didn't mean to come off that way. We haven't seen or heard from Stoney since we got knocked. Our family—you know—" My voice trailed off. Clearing my throat, I pinched the bridge of my nose.

"Look, I get it. When he left the house, the cop he thought he recognized picked him up. They sent him to juvenile detention. He called to tell me they were transferring him to an adult facility now that he's eighteen," tears rimming her eyes.

I pulled her closer, holding her hands in mine.

"You've been down since day one. We'll never forget your loyalty, ever."

Though we looked out for her, we owed her so much more.

I returned the key to her.

"Listen, if Stoney had you hold on to it, he trusted you like a muthafucka.

Shit is about to shift, and we'll be gone for at least a couple of years. We need you to keep following the path Stoney started," I told her.

She nodded. "Okay."

I walked towards the back door, stepping out onto the deck while Mookie lingered. I knew what time it was.

"We'll set up an account to make sure your shit don't stop while we're upstate. I'll call you as soon as I can. If anything happens before then, call Ant—he'll take care of it," he said while holding her hips.

When the door opened behind me, I glanced back. My brother looked sad as hell.

"Damn," I muttered.

I never saw this coming.

I tapped his chest. "You good?"

"Yeah, I'm good."

We never spoke on it again.

4

———

THE DEBT I DIDN'T OWE

At thirteen years old, my life was in shambles. I stood to my feet, not really knowing what to do about the growl in my stomach. I walked past the ugly, faded wallpaper, trailing my finger along the dirty wall until I reached the kitchen. Looking for anything—crackers, crumbs, or anything that I could eat.

My mother, Pam, used to be the coldest woman on the block. She had long, beautiful, jet-black hair, standing 5'3" and very curvaceous; her body made a lot of grown men drool. We dressed in the most expensive name-brand clothes and shoes. Men spent bands trying to outdo the last. Then she met George, a local drug dealer. We weren't rich or anything, but we were doing good. Pam had a full-time job, and I had friends. Life was good—or so I thought. Her casual drug use became a lifestyle. It didn't take long before she was hooked. She was now the neighborhood fiend.

I was also fully developed, embodying the shape of a grown woman. Looking myself over in the partially broken mirror, I sang along with Cardi B on the radio: "I make money moves, I don't gotta dance!" I swiveled my body from left to right, patting my butt.

Quick was a neighborhood boy I had a major crush on. He was a little older than me, a drug runner for one of the big-time drug lords in the neighborhood. I was embarrassed about our living conditions, so I would walk to the corner store to hook up. Never allowing him to come to our house.

When Quick noticed me standing there waiting for him, he rushed to me, kissing me all over my face. I giggled, pretending I was trying to break free.

"I'm gone make you my girl one day, watch," Quick teased, easing me a few dollars.

He liked keeping me laced because he didn't want me needing anything.

"Look, I got you something!" he said, pushing a cell phone into my hand.

I gasped.

"You got me a phone?" I said, jumping up and down. I had always wanted my own phone.

"Yeah, it's so you can call me anytime you need something."

In the beginning, I was too embarrassed. I got over that real fast. The more he came around, the more I got caught up.

I called my homegirl Keisha to tell her about my latest gift.

"You know what they say, all good things come to an end... eventually, right?" she taunted.

"Keisha, why are you trying to throw salt?" I was getting really tired of her always trying to talk down on me.

"I'm not, I promise. Ooh, girl, you are so lucky though! I can't even get a baller to look my way," she confessed.

I didn't respond. I never told her he was a baller.

"Look, Keish, I gotta go. I'm supposed to go somewhere," I lied.

"Okay, call me when you get back!"

Annoyed, I hung up. Releasing a hard breath, I slammed my body onto the mattress that was sitting on the floor. My phone vibrated. I took the call. I knew it could only be Quick.

"Hey." I smiled.

"Run through right quick."

I playfully rolled my eyes. "Come through when? Where are you?"

"Why can't you just come through?" he asked, laughing. "You know I'm at the spot, like always."

A wide smile spread across my face as I stared at the ceiling, counting the cracks, pretending to be thinking about it.

"Okay, but you know I can't stay long."

"Alright, bet! I'll see you in what... five minutes?"

"Yeah," I giggled.

Quick was older than me. He was tall and midnight dark. When he smiled, he revealed a perfect set of white teeth and was always laced in fresh gear.

Once I reached the trap house, I slowly pushed the door open.

"Quick?" I called out, reluctantly stepping inside. "You know I can't stay long. Where you at?"

The house was full of dope fiends. They were posted everywhere. The guys who ran the house with Quick were older. I never got good vibes when they were around.

Just as I turned to walk out, Quick appeared, calling my name.

"Latoya, where you going? I had to handle some shit downstairs," sounding breathy like he had been running.

"You should've been looking out for me. What were you doing?" I snapped angrily.

"Oh nah. Two crackheads were fighting downstairs."

My eyes scanned the room.

Quick motioned for me.

"Come on. I know you don't like it here, so we're going to make this fast," grabbing my hand, guiding me down the hallway.

I caught a glimpse of rooms sectioned off with sheets; a few rooms had doors.

"Where we going?" I shrieked. "I don't like it back here. It smells," I complained, squeezing his hand.

We walked to the last room with a door when he eased it open and playfully pulled me inside.

"Come on, Toya," he whispered.

I trusted him. I giggled until I stepped inside.

I gasped. "What's happening?"

Loco was sitting on the bed, chewing a toothpick. Base stood by the window with a cigarette dangling from his lips. I scanned the room in a panic.

"Quick, what's going on?" I bellowed. My voice trembled with fear.

Quick stood in the middle of the room with his arms folded, wearing a smirk.

"We found out that the crackhead who stole from us was your mother," Loco said.

"Her debt is your debt, hoe!" Base barked, stepping in my face.

"Why am I paying for her shit? Why not get it from her?"

"You're going to pay us, but we don't want money," Loco said, with hatred in his eyes.

Quick's smile faltered, but he didn't save me. He knew what they had planned. He chuckled nervously.

"Hey, come on, man, she said she ain't got nothing. Let's let her go and catch her moms when she comes back on the block."

Base smirked. "Nah, we doing this just like we said. You don't get to back out!"

Quick's betrayal stung. I really thought he cared about me.

My fear turned to rage. My voice became cold and sharp.

"Do whatever you gone do and get it over with."

Loco took two long strides and slapped me so hard I spun around, slamming against the wall.

Not giving him the satisfaction of seeing me cry, I stayed silent. I just glared at him.

When they finished, Quick trailed behind me until I reached the door.

"Toya, I'm sorry—"

"I don't want to hear it, Quick!" I barked.

When I walked away, I refused to look back.

When I reached a safe distance, I broke out into a sprint. That's when I came upon some boys playing basketball. I slowed my pace. Once I passed the ball court, I broke into a sprint until I reached our apartment.

Taking two steps at a time, barely making it to the toilet, releasing all the contents of my stomach. It wasn't much since I hadn't eaten anything.

Standing in the same broken mirror I had stood in just hours earlier, tears slowly drifted down my cheeks.

"I hate you," I hissed at my reflection. "God, why would you let this happen to me?"

I cried out, collapsing across my bed, when I felt the buzzing of my phone. I yanked it from my pocket. My hands trembled.

"What?"

"Toya, I'm sorry! I didn't know they were—"

"Shut up! Yes, you did!" I interrupted, my voice raw, filled with pain. "You knew!" My words cut through the air. "Don't ever call me again!" Then I hung up.

My body collapsed to the floor, overwhelmed by uncontrollable sobs.

5
____

THE NIGHT I MET HIM

A few years later.

The bass pounded through Club Pharaoh. Some people danced or got lost in the music, while others laughed and talked amongst friends. The energy was everything.

I moved gracefully through the crowd until I reached my friends.

"Heyyy, bitches!!!" I sang, popping my fingers and swaying my hips from side to side.

"Heyyy!!!" Chloe chimed in, swaying along with me.

We greeted each other with tight hugs.

"This place is packed. I didn't think I was ready for all this hyped energy tonight!" I said through a giggle.

"The crowd did not disappoint," Chloe chortled.

"Sure didn't. I live for this kind of energy," Mousey added.

"That's the truth," I cosigned, glancing around the club.

Trudy's eyes swept the room. "Girl, check him out! He is fine!" Our gaze followed hers to where a tall, chocolate, well-built man stood near the bar.

"He's kind of cute," Chloe said, shrugging her shoulders, sounding uninterested.

"He's not my type," Mousey chimed in. "He needs to be at least forty pounds heavier."

Causing us to erupt in laughter. When suddenly, a man standing across the room caught my attention. His gaze sent flutters throughout my body. He had a mysterious yet beautiful physique.

The night drew near, and everyone began making their way out of the club.

"I'll catch up with y'all tomorrow," I said, rendering hugs and kissing cheeks. "I'm not ready to leave just yet," silently hoping I could find that mysterious man.

"Well, don't do anything I wouldn't do," Chloe teased.

"And bitch, what would that be?" Trudy chimed in, causing us to laugh loudly.

I playfully rolled my eyes. She had a point. I always knew how to have a good time.

I lingered at the bar, sipping my drink. I scanned the room again before planning to leave, and there he was—the man from earlier, sitting at a table alone. Our eyes connected, causing my breath to catch in my chest.

This gorgeous man was tall, with broad shoulders and very confident. He was breathtaking. His dark eyes and thick brows contrasted beautifully with his almond skin. His dark eyes were spellbinding.

As our eyes locked, this time he offered me a subtle smile. I looked away as if I wasn't interested, periodically glancing behind me. He sat there, a cigar tucked between his teeth, that sexy, irresistible grin spread across his face. A low moan escaped my lips before I could catch it. I hurriedly finished my drink before tossing my jacket over my arm. When I noticed him walking towards me, his steps were slow and deliberate. I felt his presence before he said a word.

I inhaled deeply; the rich scent of Clive Christian's Imperial Majesty wrapped around me like a seductive spell. I was ready to surrender to him if he asked me to. That's how good he smelled.

Leaning against the bar, the energy between us was undeniable.

"I hope you're enjoying yourself. I'm Mario," he said against my back.

I turned and saw him—I mean really saw him. Not that he wasn't already fine, but he was even sexier up close.

"I'm Latoya, the pleasure is definitely mine. And to what do I owe this pleasure?" I flirtatiously smiled.

"Friendship."

A smirk tugged at the corners of my lips. "Oh," I said softly.

"Do you know that you're hypnotizing?" Mario asked, his tone almost serious, though a smile tugged at the corners of his lips.

"I'm sure you say that to all the ladies," I teased.

"Nah, ma, that's not my style," tilting his head slightly. "Tonight might be a little different," his gaze fixated on my lips.

"Different how?" I asked.

"It means I don't see you the same way I see most of the women who come to this club. I like what I see, Miss Latoya. I would like to get to know more about you." He paused. "If that's possible."

I didn't say anything; my smile said everything. I was flattered.

"I watched you for a while before I decided," he said.

"Decided?" I asked with a playful attitude.

"Yes, before I decided if I liked what I saw," he responded. "Will you join me for a drink?" extending his hand.

We stood face-to-face for a moment before I accepted his offer, which happened to be in VIP.

His lips were thick and succulent. His smile was beautiful, with two beautiful dimples.

His lips appeared to be moving slowly.

Wow, this man is so damn fine. And those lips... they have to be the sexiest lips I've ever seen on a man, I thought as I watched him speak.

He tilted his head slightly, meeting my gaze.

"Hello," he sang, snapping me out of my daze.

"Are your friends still here or are you here alone?" he asked a second time.

"Yes," I stammered. "I'm alone. My friends have already left," I said, attempting to reach for the empty glass that sat on the bar.

"You won't need that, love. We have plenty of drinks upstairs," he said.

"Okay," I said, leaving the empty glass on the counter.

6

DIFFERENT

It had been a long time since I felt an immediate attraction to anyone since returning home. The women I met were only interested in money, clothes, and petty shit.

I found out after I went to prison Sky moved on six months later. We were never supposed to be a long-term thing, but over time, her presence became something I depended on. I started looking forward to her letters and hearing her voice during rec.

Two weeks ago, Charlene, Sky's friend, told her she had seen me around the way, and she immediately started blowing up my phone. When I finally decided to take her call, she started in, wanting to rekindle where we left off. I couldn't trust her anymore.

"Look, Sky, I just got home," I started. "I don't want to be held down right now."

Mookie and Robert sat off in the distance, cackling like little schoolgirls as they watched me attempt to break things off.

"This bitch is delusional!" Mookie laughed, shaking his head.

I shot both of them a "shut the fuck up" look.

She was draining me, and I had just started moving around.

"I'm not saying we have to get married, Stoney. I just don't want to lose you again!" she pleaded.

"Fuck!" I barked. "I don't want to hear shit when you find out I'm fucking other bitches!" I really expected her to walk away.

But she didn't.

"Look, Stoney, just don't do it in my face. I don't want to see it or hear about it," she said.

Robert and Mookie were in disbelief.

"What the fuck?" Mookie mouthed.

Robert shook his head. "Damn," massaging his beard.

"Stoney, what the fuck you got on these girls? Who in the hell would agree to that shit!" he chortled.

"Look, my peoples here, I gotta bounce," I said before ending the call.

I could always spot the ones who were just in it for the money. Sky was starting to show those signs. Greedy. Out of nowhere, she suddenly had all of these "necessities" she expected me to take care of. Her time was already limited.

Taking Latoya by the hand, I led her upstairs to the VIP area. I'm not sure why I gravitated towards her. Trusting anyone outside my family was never something I felt comfortable with, but her vibe was different—so different, I felt drawn to know more about her.

Mookie and Robert were posted nearby, observing the patrons who entered the VIP area.

Mookie had a beautiful woman sitting on his lap, another woman chilling on the arm of his chair.

Mario entered the room. "Everyone, this beautiful young lady to my left is Latoya; she's my guest this evening."

Their eyes shifted towards Latoya. She nervously smiled as she stood next to Mario.

"She is definitely a beauty, Stone. I'm Money. I'm this foo's brother," he said, tossing a nod towards Mario.

Mookie introduced himself and the others followed.

"Okay—okay, y'all trying to steal my girl?" he teased. "Y'all some sneaky niggas," Mario joked, causing everyone to laugh.

Turning to Latoya, sweeping my hand over the room.

"You can trust any man in this room. Nothing goes down without them knowing," I told her with confidence.

"You were alone downstairs; where were they then?" she asked.

"Baby, I'm never alone—even when it looks like it," placing a peck on her neck.

The night went over perfectly. The chemistry between us was undeniable.

"I'm really feeling this time getting to know you, Ms. Toya," I whispered, causing her to snuggle closer into my shoulder.

"Really?" she whispered.

"Yeah, really," I said as I pressed a soft kiss to her lips.

7

THE MORNING AFTER

Last night was a blur. One minute I was laughing, talking, and dancing with Mario and his family, having the time of my life —to waking up in an unfamiliar place.

Stirring beneath the covers, I stretched and yawned before my eyes fluttered open. "Wait—where am I?" I asked aloud, though no one was around.

"Good morning, beautiful," a deep baritone voice rumbled from the side of the bed.

I blinked quickly, trying to focus, scanning the room. Squinting—one eye open—I found the most beautiful smile looking down at me.

"Good morning," I replied groggily.

"I wasn't sure if you drink coffee or not, but you could definitely use some after last night," he said, grinning, revealing a mouth full of perfect teeth.

I offered a half-smile, clearing my throat. "Thank you."

He sat on the bed near my feet. "Do you feel like you have a hangover?"

I shook my head. "No."

Smiling, he said, "Then you should be able to eat breakfast. Come down when you're ready. I'll grab you a set of towels so you can wash your face—and any other part of your body you decide to wash."

His teasing made me laugh.

"Oh, so she does smile," he teased.

"Of course I smile," I shot back jokingly.

I accepted the towels, along with a newly packaged toothbrush, and headed into the bathroom. I took a quick shower and brushed my teeth before heading downstairs.

The aroma drifting through the air was mouthwatering. When I reached the bottom of the stairs, Mario was standing at the stove, stirring something in a pot.

"Hey."

He turned to face me. "Hey, you're just in time. Do you like grits?"

"Grits? I think I had them once, it's been a while."

He flashed that handsome smile again.

"Well, these grits," he said, pointing at the pot and smacking his lips, "are the best grits in this area... no... in the entire world!"

We both burst into laughter.

His jokes allowed me to relax. He set two places at the peninsula, then poured each of us a cup of coffee.

My eyes wandered around his house, taking in every detail. The kitchen was breathtaking, spacious yet modern, with a marble countertop that stretched across the entire island. Dark oak cabinets contrasted beautifully with a deep bluish-grey backsplash, and state-of-the-art appliances completed the look. Everything was perfectly coordinated.

"I can give you a tour after we eat?" he offered.

"Okay."

He leaned in, pecking me softly on my lips before sitting down. It caught me off guard.

When he kissed me, my heart fluttered. He gently placed his hand over mine.

"You good?"

I nodded. He said a quick prayer before we ate, impressing me even more. My eyes traced the sharp line of his jawbone. Every feature on his face seemed to be carved with perfection. The first time I saw him, he appeared untouchable. And here I was sharing breakfast with this man.

He kept his word and showed me every room in his house. When we reached his bedroom, he grinned.

"This is the best room in the entire house!"

"How is that?" I asked, arching my brow.

"This room is where all the magic happens!" he teased.

I playfully shoved his shoulder. "Shut up!" I giggled.

When we were done, he turned to face me.

"So, what does your schedule look like for the rest of the week? I'd ask you out again, but—" giving me a playful smile, "I don't have your number."

I may have paused a little too long, because he crouched slightly, meeting my gaze.

"Does that mean you don't want me to have it?" he joked, his brows knitted.

"Yes, I want you to have it—if you're actually going to use it," I smiled.

A wide smile spread across his face as he pulled me into his arms, one hand resting gently around my waist.

Clearing his throat, he repeated his question, this time in a playful tone.

"Ma, may I please have your number?"

"Yes," I giggled as we exchanged numbers.

8

CAUGHT SLIPPING

I walked Latoya to her car, feeling like a simp for actually hoping she'd call. It had been a while since I cared whether a woman reached out or not. I usually kept two or three women in rotation. No strings attached.

Latoya was different, proving that each time we hung out.

When I got back inside, my cell phone was ringing. I didn't rush to answer it because the only person I wanted to talk to had just left my house.

I strolled over to my phone and glanced at the missed call. "Money, I'll call him back," I mumbled. I was a gentle giant when it came to someone I cared about, and I didn't want him to notice. Not yet. He would tell Mookie, and they would clown me every chance they got. I laughed to myself when I thought about the time they caught me slipping with Kori in high school. That girl had a nigga wide open. When I told her how I felt, she laughed in my face. I never told my brothers. I brushed it off like it was a joke, but that shit hit hard. I swore that would never happen to me again.

My phone started ringing again. I didn't check the caller ID; instead, I swiped to answer.

"What, nigga?" I laughed.

"Hello?" A soft voice. Her voice.

"I'm sorry—I thought you were my brother," I told her, clearing my throat. "Shit!" I mouthed.

She paused.

"What's up, Toy?" I asked, giving her a nickname the night we met.

"I made it home and wanted to let you know. And who said you could call me Toya?" she laughed.

"You already know—I do what I want," I joked.

"Oh, you do?" she giggled.

Her voice ran through my mind all day, every day. I hadn't been able to stop thinking about her since she left my house. I was getting caught up, and I couldn't understand how.

"I was hoping to see you again. When can we make that happen?" I asked.

What is wrong with you? I mouthed, slapping my forehead.

"I really had a good time the other night. Watching you try to dance was kind of cute," she teased.

"Ma, I got all the moves—why you playing?" I teased before shifting the conversation.

"Let me take you out?"

"Okay, when?"

"What about Saturday? And before you say anything, I'll get your address by the end of the week—or you can give it to me now."

She laughed before giving me her address. I felt good, and that's something I hadn't felt in a long time.

When my phone began to ring again, this time I checked the caller ID.

"What's poppin'?" I called out.

"What it do?" Mookie shot back.

"Bruh, I just answered my phone a second ago thinking it was you or Money—and it was ole girl from the club!"

"Word?"

"Word."

"Damn, I know you were hella embarrassed," he laughed.

"I was!" I laughed before shifting the conversation. "We need to hook up soon—face to face."

"Alright. When?" he asked.

"This week. I'll loop Money in."

"Cool!" Mookie said before disconnecting.

Mookie was from a dysfunctional family that always seemed to be knee-deep in other people's shit. When we got sent upstate, his family disappeared by the time he got home—no word, no trace, nothing. When he showed up to an empty house, it hit him hard. Robert's mother, Danielle, whom we affectionately called Ma Dee, allowed us to stay with them. She gave us more than a place to stay— she gave us a family again.

"Aww nah, I know you're not in love already!" He fell over laughing. "Aye Money, this nigga in love—already!"

"Hold up, nigga, I'm not in love!"

"But is she cool though?"

"Yeah, she's real cool."

"That's what's up. She was pretty as hell, I know that much."

"Look, fool—I don't have ugly friends!"

"Now that's a lie!" He roared with laughter. "That one girl, Sky—now she was ugly!"

I heard Robert snatch the phone.

"What up, Bruh?"

"I can't call it. What up with it?"

"Got word there's a problem at the Dungeon. Some fool trying to finesse."

"Word?"

Our name carried weight. Everybody knew how we got down.

"I'll get Rosco to check it out."

Pops ran the south side of DC for nearly two decades. By the time we reached twenty-one and were out on the streets, we were ready to take over where he left off. Pops said the game had changed. There wasn't any honor in it anymore. He decided to go legit, taking a job at the Post Office. Said he slept better at night.

We didn't get it then. We were young and in love with the streets. He looked me in my eyes.

"What have you boys been up to?"

"We've been running the restaurant and clubs," I said, rubbing my hand down my beard.

"Hmph," he grunted.

"We're straight, Pops," I said, holding his gaze. "I promise. We've followed every word down to the tee when it comes to putting in work."

"I hope that includes getting out these streets," he said. "I don't want you having to watch your back every time you leave your house. It's time for all of you to find a good woman and settle down." He chuckled. "Me and your mother want some grandbabies to chase around this big ole house."

I nodded. A few minutes later, Robert and Mookie joined us by the fire pit.

"What's happening over here?" Robert joked.

"Everything good?" Mookie asked, stepping around Robert.

"Yeah," Pops chuckled, "just chatting it up with Stoney, telling him your mama and I need y'all to settle down."

Mookie raised his hands in mock surrender. "I'm good, Pops," causing us to laugh.

"Pops, ask Stoney how close he is to meeting that demand," Robert chortled.

Pops side-eyed me. "You mean to tell me after all I said, you couldn't tell me?" he laughed, raising a playful fist.

Grinning, I hugged him. "I love you, Pops. That's straight from a king's heart. I'll introduce her soon, properly."

Pops nodded. "I know you will," patting me on my back.

Then he pointed at Mookie and Robert. "Find somebody like Stoney. Maybe we can get some little feet running around here again. Bring life back into this house."

Mookie widened his eyes and pointed at Robert. "Not me, fam—he's talking about you."

"Nah, he had the right person the first time." Robert dragged his hand down his beard, tossing his head my way.

As we walked to our cars, Mookie called out.

"I'll be home watching the game if y'all want to stop through. But know this is Steelers territory!" Mookie teased.

I grabbed my phone from the holder and dialed Latoya. I couldn't wait to talk to her.

"Hello," she answered. Her voice was so soft and sweet.

"Hey, you," I smiled, even though she couldn't see me.

She had me falling—and I was falling hard.

"How did it go at your parents'?"

"It's always a good time when I see them. Moms threw down, so you know I ate," I joked.

"Greedy," she teased.

I took a deep breath, feeling the weight of my thoughts. She made me ready to do things differently. Ready to let someone in. Let her in.

"Are you making your way to me tonight?" I asked, really wanting to see her.

"Yeah, if you want me to."

"Look, I want to see you. Is that cool?"

"Yes, I want to see you too," she giggled.

Yep. Things were definitely looking up.

9

———

TOO GOOD TO BE REAL

Sitting on the sofa, my feet tucked beneath me with my phone pressed to my ear.

"You will not believe what happened after y'all left Club Pharaoh," I said, feeling giddy.

"What happened? Wait—we haven't been there in a minute!" Chloe replied.

"I know," I giggled. "I had to test the waters before I let my girls in on it," I laughed.

"Yeah, right!" Chloe laughed. "So, what happened?"

I told her everything—from meeting Mario to waking up in his bed the next morning and that we had been pretty much inseparable. It's been months, and I swear it's scaring me. It's almost too perfect.

"Don't you think it's too early for us to spend that much time together?"

"Not really."

"Well, I'm practically living at his place!" I whispered, even though I knew I was alone.

"Girl!" she said, dragging the word. "Wow, this is new for you! A boyfriend? Girl, I'm happy for you!"

In the past, relationships and I didn't mix. The idea scared me when it all came down to me trusting him to be there when my own mother wasn't.

"Damn," I sighed. "How do I move forward so I don't mess this one up?" My voice cracked. I was for real scared! "It feels like this could really be something good, and I don't want to sabotage it, Chloe," I said through a tearful whisper.

"I get it, boo," she said empathetically. "I know you're confused by your feelings right now—I get it. Look, let's get together with the girls this weekend," she suggested. "Kind of like we used to do in college."

"Okay," I reluctantly agreed, because I definitely needed an intervention before I lost this man.

"I love you!" she sang into the phone.

I held back more tears when I managed to croak out, "I love you too."

Pulling together a few pieces of clothes from my closet, I packed an overnight bag. Sitting on my bed, I drew in a nervous breath. *Here goes nothing,* I muttered. Tonight, I needed to feel this man. Everything in me was telling me to run. Fear had always been a huge part of my life, masked by confidence. I had never been in love before, but if this is what it felt like, I wanted it every single day.

I tossed my bag into the back seat of my car, then hopped into the driver's seat. Starting the car, I dialed Mario. His phone went straight to voicemail, causing my chest to tighten. My past insecurities were creeping back into my life, causing me to panic. I immediately became anxious.

"Please, please, please answer," I whispered, tapping my fingers nervously on the steering wheel.

"Hey, baby," he answered in a breathy tone.

"What were you doing? Why are you so out of breath?" sounding almost accusatory.

"Come again?" His tone was sharp.

I slammed my head against the headrest, releasing the breath I had been unknowingly holding. I knew immediately, this was my bullshit starting up all over again.

"I'm just making sure I didn't interrupt anything," I said, trying hard to get back on track.

"I was downstairs, and my phone was upstairs," he said; his tone was no longer harsh, yet firm. Then he softened. "Look, I can't wait to see you. I was getting things together before you got here. I don't want you seeing me living like a slob already!" he teased, causing me to laugh.

"I'm just leaving my house. I should be there in a few minutes."

10

MR. JOHNSON

Bistro was one of the finest restaurants in the heart of the city. I paced through the dining area in a tailored charcoal suit, gold watch glinting under the lights. Beneath my polished exterior, my past life as a feared drug lord was well known around our city.

We had been trying to retire from "the drug business," choosing instead to pursue other entrepreneurial interests. But the undercurrent of our old world ran through our veins and, at times, our interactions with the restaurant employees unnerved the intensity of my past.

"Tony!" I called out sharply; my voice cut through the busyness of the kitchen. Tony, the head chef, looked up from his station where he was folding ribbons of fresh pasta.

"Yeah, boss?" Tony's hands paused, his face guarded.

I walked briskly toward him, my polished shoes clicking against the tiled floor. I picked up a plate from the counter, holding it at arm's length. "What is this?" I asked; my tone was stern but sounded calm.

Tony wiped his hands nervously on his apron. "It's today's special, Mr. Johnson. Made up just like you wanted."

I set the plate down with a deliberate thud. "Just like I wanted? Just like I wanted?" My voice rose just enough to make the other employees freeze. "Tony, this dish looks like it's been slapped together by someone who learned to cook in a gas station."

"But—"

"But what? No buts!" I tapped my finger on the marble counter. "Presentation, Tony. Presentation is everything. You think a customer is going to pay what we charge for something that looks like it fell off the back of a truck?"

Tony swallowed hard, nodding. "I'll fix it, Mr. Johnson. I'll fix it."

"Good." I leaned in close, my voice dropping to a low murmur that only Tony could hear. "Because if you don't, you might find yourself cooking meals in your mother's basement."

Meanwhile, out in the dining area, Kira, the lead restaurant manager, was rearranging menus when I approached her. She straightened up immediately, flashing a bright smile.

"Kira, how's the floor looking tonight?" I asked; my tone was oddly pleasant.

"We've got three large reservations, Mr. Johnson," she replied crisply. "A corporate party, a celebrity birthday party, and a private table reservation in the VIP."

I nodded approvingly, but then my sharp eyes caught the faintest smudge on the wine glasses lined up at the bar. My smile vanished.

"Linda," I said slowly, pointing toward the smudged glasses. "What's this? Fingerprints? Smudges? You think my guests are going to toast with a glass that looks like it was washed in the Hudson River?"

Linda's cheeks flushed. "I—I'll handle it right now, Mr. Johnson."

"You better," I said, my voice like a velvet-coated razor blade. "Because here at Bistro, we don't do sloppy. Alright?"

"Yes, Mr. Johnson. I understand."

Later that evening, as the dinner rush began, I wandered into the back, where a new dishwasher named Jermaine was quickly scrubbing pans as if his life depended on it.

"Jermaine," I said, startling him. Water splashed over the edge of the sink as Jermaine spun around.

"Yes, sir?"

I watched him for a minute; my expression was unreadable. "You're the new guy, right? You like it here?"

"It's great here, sir. I like it a lot, sir." Jermaine's voice trembled slightly.

"Good." I picked up a clean plate from the drying rack, inspecting it closely. "You know, Jermaine, in my line of work—past line of work, I should say—little details could mean the difference between... well, between everything and nothing. You understand what I'm saying?"

Jermaine nodded vigorously, though he wasn't entirely sure he understood.

"Good. So, keep those dishes spotless, and you'll do just fine." I clapped him on the shoulder with a bit of force that made Jermaine wobble slightly. "Welcome to the family."

By the end of the night, the chaos had subsided, and the restaurant buzzed with the softer sounds of clinking glasses and muffled conversations. I stood by the front door, watching the employees with a sense of pride on how well things were going. It had been a long night.

As the last guests departed and the restaurant closed for the night, one thing was clear: at Bistro, the food was exquisite, the service impeccable, and everything ran like a well-oiled machine. I demanded perfection when it came to the restaurant.

I called a meeting for first thing in the morning to address some upcoming changes and a few issues I observed during the lunch and dinner rush. During a team meeting, Linda caught my attention with a flirty smile and a soft, almost seductive tone.

"Um, Mr. Johnson, I have a question."

"Go ahead, Ms. Linda. What's on your mind?" returning the smile.

She batted her long lashes, eyes hooded with a playful look. "What if I need to reach you and you're not around?"

She smiled again, and I matched it before leaning forward.

"There are enough managers on duty who can handle any and all situations that may come up," I said, tapping the table for emphasis. "With that, are there any concerns that need my immediate attention?"

Before Linda could respond, I addressed the room.

"Managers, if there's anything the staff need, please handle it swiftly. If it's something you need approval for or something you're unable to resolve, reach out to the upper management team."

All the managers nodded, letting me know they understood the assignment. The meeting wrapped up, and the staff began clearing the room.

Kira stayed behind.

Now Kira, she was something else. Built like a replica of Beyoncé, curves in all the right places. I'd heard from the other staff that she was an Insta model. Wouldn't even be surprised if she had a Fans Only page.

"Hey, Kira, what's up?" I asked casually.

She bit her bottom lip, catching it between her teeth. "Mr. Johnson, when are you going to let me cook for you?" she asked in a sultry tone.

I tilted my head. "Cook for me? I wasn't aware you knew your way around a kitchen like that," I said, genuinely surprised.

She leaned in slightly; her voice was low and sultry. "There's a lot about me you don't know, Mr. Johnson."

I cleared my throat. "Now that, you're right about. Sure, you can show off your cooking skills with the staff. I'm sure they would like that."

She looked at me with narrowed eyes. "The staff?" she scoffed. "I'm trying to cook for two," her tone was firm and direct.

A slow smile spread across my face. "Well, that can't happen, Kira. My woman would feel some type of way about being left out."

As I walked away, I shook my head, smirking. *Damn... why is she coming at me like that now? A few months ago, it could've went down just like that.*

I left her standing there, a mischievous grin plastered on her face.

11

THIRTY-SIX MONTHS

Life was never easy for me. My mother worked two jobs, but even with her grinding, we struggled to make ends meet, often lacking stability along the way. By the time I was fifteen, I had already experienced serious hardships, including abandonment by my pops, experiences that shaped my view of the world and made it hard for me to trust anyone. I became a product of my environment. I started running dope for one of the top drug lords in our neighborhood.

It wasn't long before my friends were running with me. We made more money in a week than my mother made in a month working both jobs. She refused the money I tried giving her, calling it "the devil's money" and wanted no parts of it. I didn't argue about it. Instead, I paid her bills before they ever hit the mailbox.

Mookie lived in the projects, and my mother rented a house that wasn't far from the projects. Robert's family was doing well. I didn't know where Mr. B worked; I just knew he made a lot of money, and they lived in a big-ass house out in the suburbs. We went to the same schools from elementary through high school, often sharing the same classes. That's how we met and became close.

One night changed our lives forever. We witnessed a man murdered by his wife's lover. The husband was driving down dark streets searching for his wife. When he spotted her walking hand in hand with her lover, he jumped out of his car to confront them. His wife tried to calm him down, but he was too angry. Swinging at the lover, he landed a couple of punches, but when he went to swing again, he found himself staring down the barrel of a Tec-9. The lover pulled the trigger, shooting him point-blank in the head.

The lover dropped his gun, leaving his terrified lover and three teenagers as witnesses. I was supposed to be in bed that night, but I often snuck out through my window to meet up with Robert and Akeem, whom we called Mookie. I didn't realize at the time how that night would change my life.

The boldness in that man's eyes before he pulled the trigger became a symbol of power for me. I grew to be fearless, ruthless, and cold. We dove headfirst into the game. As promised, Pops handed us the reins when he felt we were ready; we methodically extended our territory and maintained absolute control.

We never allowed outsiders because too many had bitten the hand that fed them. Anyone brought into the fold had to be vetted by all of us. We were equals. Falling in love wasn't out of the question; if it happened, it happened. Understand that loyalty was everything in this game. Betrayal was never tolerated!

I thought back to the day I lost three years of my life. Sitting next to my attorney, I folded my hands in front of me, staring at the dull grey walls that surrounded us. The atmosphere in the courtroom was cold and harsh.

At the time of my arrest, Mookie, Money, and I were preparing to attend Morehouse. My mother's dreams for me were to finish college and land a good job. Although she had lived an amazing life with my father, she wanted me to live a better life than they had.

The gavel struck sharply, calling the courtroom to order. Judge Daniels, a man in his late fifties with silver-streaked hair and a commanding presence, adjusted his glasses and peered down at the documents in front of him. He'd overseen the case for weeks, and the strain showed in his tired eyes.

"Mr. Johnson," he began, his voice low and deliberate. "You have been found guilty of unlawful possession of a firearm. Before I pronounce your sentence, do you wish to say anything?"

My throat was dry as hell. I cleared my throat as I stood. "Your Honor, I've made some mistakes, but Your Honor, my family and I live in a rough neighborhood. Carrying a firearm wasn't my best choice, but at the time, I believed I had to carry it for my protection."

The prosecutor, Gracie Moore, a well-put-together woman in her mid-forties with a no-nonsense demeanor, stood to respond. "Your Honor, while we acknowledge the defendant's remorse, the law must still be upheld. Illegal firearm possession threatens public safety. We request a sentence that reflects this gravity."

I could feel their eyes on me. Their unspoken judgment was hanging thick in the air. The worry showing on my mother's face caused my heart to drop. Marcellous sat beside her, struggling to stay composed. Judge Daniels glanced at me one last time, then looked out across the courtroom.

"Mr. Johnson, your expressed remorse and clean record are noted. But the law is unambiguous. Our community's safety must come first. For unlawful possession of a firearm, you are sentenced to thirty-six months in the State Penitentiary. Upon release, you will complete two hundred hours of community service and serve two years' probation. This sentence aims to balance accountability with a chance for reha-bilitation."

My heart plummeted—thirty-six months. I watched my family as I fought back tears.

"Court is adjourned," the judge said, striking the gavel one final time.

The courtroom stirred as people stood. My attorney, Mr. Dawson, leaned in before the bailiff led me out of the room. "We'll appeal his ruling and explore every option available. It's not over, Mario."

I barely registered his words. "Thirty-six months" echoed in my head. I was full of regret, anger, and shame all at the same damn time. Thankful Marcellous chose to keep India away from the trial.

This whole situation screamed setup. Betrayal was a bitch!

Sitting up in bed, my breathing caught in my chest, I reached for my phone and dialed a familiar number.

"Hey, Ma."

12

COME STAY WITH ME

I finished my shower and began getting ready for bed when my phone vibrated. I swiped the flashing green bar.

"Hello?"

"Hey, Ma," he replied.

"Hey! Everything okay?"

"Yeah, everything's good. What you doing right now?" he asked.

"Getting ready for bed. What's up?"

"Come stay with me tonight."

My heart fluttered. "Tonight?" A little confused by the sudden request.

"Is that cool? I need to see you," he said.

"Give me a few minutes and I'll be there."

I quickly packed an overnight bag and headed over to Mario's. When I arrived, he met me at my car, and as soon as I stepped out, he pulled me into a tight embrace for what felt like forever.

I pulled away to gaze into his eyes. "Hey, what's wrong?"

Shaking his head, he pecked my lips before tossing my duffle bag over his shoulder. "I missed you," he said gently as he held my waist, walking me inside.

Once we settled in, I joined him at the peninsula.

"Baby, what's wrong? Did something happen?"

He walked over to me, wrapping his arms around me. He felt more relaxed now.

"I just had some shit on my mind and couldn't sleep. For some reason, your worrisome ass brings me comfort," he chortled.

I playfully shoved him. "Shut up!" I said through giggles.

Causing him to laugh before kissing my forehead.

"I missed you too," I admitted. "I'll always be there when you need me," I whispered.

"I need you right now in the worst way," he whispered, catching his lip between his teeth. Heat surged between my thighs. Yeah, this was going to be a long night.

ACT II

LOVE UNDER PRESSURE

13

LIVING TOGETHER

I had been staying at Mario's house for about three months now. I tried calling him several times before finally giving up.

I really think I screwed up this time, I muttered to myself. We kept butting heads. I had never lived with a man before, and I wasn't sure how this was supposed to go. I also didn't know how to handle the late hours he often worked.

It was five thirty a.m. when I heard keys turning in the lock. Sitting up in bed, I was unsure how I should feel. Should I be relieved he came home after staying out all night—or angry that it took him so long to get here?

For the first time, I was overwhelmed by my emotions. I couldn't understand it. Vulnerability had never been a safe place for me. We'd been together for almost a year. One thing my life taught me was that love, especially from a man, came with a price. Hell, I couldn't even trust my own mother, so how could I trust a man?

"Hey," he called out softly as he stepped through the threshold of our bedroom.

"Hey," my body shifting. Feeling guarded.

He sat at the foot of the bed, his eyes low as he undressed quietly. I watched him carefully, searching for signs of regret, distance, or the slightest sign I needed to prepare for bad news.

"Mario, where were you?" I whispered.

He placed his shoes neatly in the closet, right beside his sweatsuits. That little act was so ordinary, it still made me pause. His attention to detail, the way he took care of himself, was one of the many things I adored about him.

"I went to my brother's," he groaned. His gaze locked on me. "Listen, I don't want to keep fighting. Baby, are we good?"

I wanted to say yes. I wanted to believe we were good. "I—I think so," I whispered, my voice shaky. I wasn't sure.

I begged myself. "Don't cry, Latoya. Don't you dare cry."

He reached out gently, cupping my chin.

"Baby, what's wrong?"

"I'm glad you're home. I don't want to fight with you either."

Even when things weren't perfect between us, he still showed me he cared. I didn't know what to do with that kind of tenderness. Knowing I could lose this both settled and terrified me.

"I'm not sure where we're headed," he said, his voice low. "But I know we need to be on the same team," he said firmly.

"Baby, I am on your team. I really am. But this is new for me. You're the first man in my life who hasn't hurt me."

That truth broke something in me. I couldn't hold it in anymore. The tears flooded my face.

He pulled me into his arms without hesitation. "Baby, I never want to be the reason you cry. You mean the world to me—and I don't think you understand how much that means to a nigga like me."

I pulled back just enough to look in his eyes. "No one's ever cared about me like this, not even Pam."

I kissed him passionately. I needed him to feel what I couldn't say. I loved him.

And he did.

That night wasn't like anything I'd ever known. There was nothing transactional, nothing performative. It wasn't about our bodies intermingling; it was about healing. We held each other like we were trying to unlearn everything we'd been taught about love.

Before Mario, Lydia and Grandma Louise were the only people who held my heart. I'd never known love like this from a man.

Mario made ordinary things feel extraordinary. He listened when I rambled, complimented me when I didn't feel pretty, always said please and thank you. I didn't realize how much those small things mattered until he entered my life.

That night, I stopped trying to be strong, and I let him love me the way he'd always tried to. And for the first time, I didn't push it away.

After we made love, our bodies still intertwined in the dark, he brushed a strand of hair from my face and looked at me like I was the only woman in the world.

"You trying to make a nigga fall in love?" he asked with a soft chuckle.

I looked away, unsure how to answer him. "What does love look like?" I asked, barely above a whisper.

He didn't say anything. Maybe he didn't need to. Maybe what we had in that moment was the answer.

14

TEN TOES DOWN

The next morning, the aroma of breakfast pulled me from my sleep. Smiling, I hurried downstairs.

"Mmm," I moaned. "That smells delicious!"

Mario turned from the stove, flashing his handsome smile.

"You better believe a brother can get down in the kitchen!"

He grabbed two plates from the cabinet, loading them with French toast, fried potatoes, bacon, and scrambled eggs. On my way to the table, I snagged a strip of bacon from the tray.

"Okay, I see you, Chef Mario," I giggled.

He poured two mugs of hot, steamy coffee and set them on the table before returning with our plates. As he sat across from me, he peered over the rim of his cup. My eyes were still heavy with sleep, my simple curls pinned back into a messy ponytail.

Clearing his throat, he spoke gently. "How are you doing this morning?"

I smirked, peering over my mug. "It's barely seven in the morning, but I'm good."

Mario poured syrup over his French toast, his voice sounding more serious.

"Toya, we need to talk about last night."

Causing my smile to falter. Feeling vulnerable, I lowered my gaze.

"Why?" I murmured. "We made beautiful love last night, so what is there to talk about? Unless..." Giving him a faint, uneasy smile before rising from the table and clearing my plate.

Mario remained seated at the island, watching my every move. I headed upstairs to shower.

Once upstairs, I carried my towel into the bathroom, turning on the shower. As steam curled in the air, I slipped out of my robe. I caught a quick glimpse of myself in the full-length mirror. I froze.

My eyes tracked every scar, each mark. Each one carried a memory. And just like that, I was back there again.

My hands clenched the edge of the counter as I shut my eyes, visions of Mr. George's rage flooding back—blood trickling across his cheek from the scratch I'd given him. The memory overwhelmed me.

"Bitch, you scratched my face!" he barked, hurling me to the floor.

He repeatedly stomped me. I curled into myself, trying to absorb the blows.

"Mr. George!" I screamed. "I'm sorry! Please!"

I prayed Pam would bust through the door to save me.

But no one came.

I gripped the sink, slowly shaking my head from side to side as soft sobs escaped my lips.

"Who could love somebody like me?" I whimpered.

I stood there until I was able to regain my composure. Stepping inside the shower, I welcomed the water spraying over my face; it was as if the water could wash away all of my pain.

Mario soon joined me.

"I miss this with you," he whispered, kissing the back of my neck.

I melted at his touch as I released a soft moan.

"You're going to make me late," I giggled, my giggles soon fading into soft moans as I rested my leg on the edge of the shower bench, steam curling around me as water traced a lazy path down my body. Mario leaned his body into mine; his touch was gentle, two fingers gliding slowly along my center before easing inside me. My breath hitched, a moan slipping free as my body arched toward him, trembling under the weight of the sensation.

He didn't rush. He explored me like a secret he already knew but wanted to memorize again, inch by tender inch.

I felt his arousal pressing against my thigh, his breath warm against my skin as he leaned into me, his lips brushing across my ear.

"I love you, Toya," he whispered.

My heart fluttered, but I didn't answer.

I couldn't.

I held my eyes closed, allowing myself to feel his words.

"Toya, did you hear me? Talk to me," he panted.

"Mario, you already know how I feel," I moaned. "We talked about this last night," I said, unintentionally changing the mood. My voice was low, pleading for him not to push for more.

"I need to know my girl is ten toes down for me. I need to feel it, Toya."

"Mario, despite what it may look like, I am down for you!" I sighed as I stepped out of the shower, frustrated by the continued push.

Mario quickly finished his shower, wrapping a towel around his waist. He briskly walked into the bedroom, hoping to catch me before I left.

But the room was already empty.

15

—————

WHAT I NEVER TOLD YOU

Thoughts of Pam flooded my mind out of nowhere. I wondered if she was dead or alive. Several years and no one had heard from her. Not once did she think to call me or Lydia! I turned to face Chloe; my frustration was bubbling over.

"Does she even think about us?"

I glanced away, struggling to hold back my tears.

Lydia had moved to Detroit, leaving Grandma Louise behind in Lafayette. She was married with three beautiful girls, each one just as stunning as she was. Turning back to Chloe, "I tried to get her out of Louisiana, you know?"

Chloe remained quiet, allowing me the space to vent.

"After college, I begged her to move to Virginia with me, but she'd fallen in love with Richard." My voice drifting, staring off into the distance. "I wanted her to be happy. To have a better life than we did as children," I continued.

"I noticed that you've been down lately. Is that why?" Chloe asked.

I nodded. "I miss them, a lot," I whispered as I swiped a tear from my cheek. "I call her every month just to check in. You know what she says? 'They're fine, she's just cooking and cleaning!'" I raised my brow, displaying a goofy expression.

We burst into a fit of giggles, remembering how we used to bribe Lydia in order for her to clean her side of the room.

"I'm sure she's fine," Chloe said.

"Yeah, I know. It's just..." My voice trailed off. "Growing up, I felt like I needed to protect her more than anything. I'd do anything to keep her safe—even if it meant letting men have their way with me, as long as they left her alone."

Chloe jerked her head towards me, her eyes widened in shock. "What?"

"Don't, Chloe. Please don't look at me like that. I'm okay. That was a long time ago."

After a few minutes of heavy silence had passed, instantly regretting my slip-up.

"Maybe I should just go back home and allow things to blow over."

"No, Toya. Please don't go," she said, as she jumped to her feet. "I'm not judging you, I'm really not. It's just—I was just caught off guard. And this was the first time I heard this story. Please stay," Chloe pleaded.

Reluctantly, I nodded. Chloe walked over to the refrigerator, pulling out a bottle of wine, pouring both of us a glass.

"So," I said, attempting to change the mood, "tell me about the man who has all of your attention." I smiled hard. "I'm glad you found somebody."

"He's so nice," Chloe beamed. "At first, I was scared he would be like all those crazy men I dated in the past, but he's not like them at all!"

"So, have you two been out on a date yet?"

Before she could respond, her phone buzzed; Robert's name flashed across the screen. She turned, facing me with a huge smile, and silently mouthed, "It's him," pointing at her phone.

She pranced into the living room. When she came back into the room, she announced that Robert was having a cookout and he was inviting her friends. The timing was perfect. She was so happy. Mario's face flashed through my mind; I missed my man. I stood, quickly gathering my things.

"Chloe, that sounds great," I said, rushing towards the door, "but I think I'm going to head home. Text me the details, okay?" And with that, I was out the door.

16

———

LOVE DON'T LIVE HERE ANYMORE

Revisiting my childhood home in Jamaica, Queens, NY. I swore I would never return following my release from prison.

Dressed in a silk chocolate Armani suit and tie, wearing a pair of Dior shoes, and with a custom-made Italian wool Balmacaan trench coat draped over my arm, I felt somewhat out of place.

"MJ?"

I spun quickly towards the sound, my brows tightly knitted.

"Who's asking?"

No response. Instead, the figure stepped into view.

Instinctively, I placed my hand on my piece. But then he raised his hands in front of him.

"Wait a minute, young blood."

I paused, narrowing my eyes.

"Who's asking?" I repeated slowly.

"Rufus. Your neighbor."

My brows knitted deeper, eyes squinting.

"Mr. Rufus?"

He nervously chuckled.

"I almost didn't recognize you." His tone relaxed now that I acknowledged him.

I relaxed too.

"I'm sorry, Mr. Rufus, can't be too sure who's out here anymore," I said in a softer tone.

He nodded.

"Yeah, I know. I didn't expect to see you around here anymore. Once you left, your mother, sister, and your brother moved away."

My jaw tightened.

"Yeah, I know."

The memory of coming home to an empty house washed over me; the feeling of abandonment instantly consumed me.

"Listen, Mr. Rufus, I don't want to be rude, but I have to go," I said, turning my back to him, not wanting him to see the pain in my eyes.

"Before you go, young blood, I need to show you something. Ride with me right quick?"

Not really in the mood, I tried declining, but he was persistent.

"Okay," I finally agreed.

He drove for several miles. Unsure of where we were heading, I blurted, "Where are you going?"

Now on high alert, I remained silent. Minutes later, we pulled into a cemetery.

"What are we doing here?" Anxiety prickled my skin.

He stepped out, walked to my door, and opened it. Confused, I stepped out.

Placing a hand on my shoulder, he lowered his eyes.

"Follow me, it's not far."

I took slow, methodical steps, my stomach knotting tighter with every step.

Mr. Rufus stopped at a flat headstone covered by grass. Placing his hand on my shoulder, he spoke again, a little more cautiously.

"Son, not long after you left, your mother had a stroke. She was placed in a nursing home for about six months. Once she was released, your sister took her home with her so she could care for her. I'd say not even a year later, someone broke into their house and..."

I grabbed my chest and fell to my knees. A sad reality hit me—had I been home, I could've been there for them.

"My brother, where's my brother?" I managed to croak out.

"It was only your mother and sister. Your brother wasn't there."

Mr. Rufus gave me time to grieve before yet again placing his hand on my shoulder, which was now rising and falling as I could no longer hold back my tears.

When I left Mr. Rufus, I called my brothers and told them everything. My brothers and I vowed to find those niggas who killed my family. I wanted revenge.

17

THE PAST ISN'T FINISHED

I sat slouched at my desk, debating whether to hit Club Pharaoh or keep it low-key for the evening, when my phone vibrated.

"Hi Robert, I know it's been a while, but can we talk? Vanessa."

Her message was displayed across my screen, interrupting my vibe. She was someone I wanted to forget. Forget how she dissed me when I was sent upstate. My fingers hovering over my phone, as flashbacks to the last time we were face-to-face at the trial before I was sentenced. She promised she would wait for me, but not long after arriving, her letters were dwindling down to nothing. The feeling wasn't something you could plan for, but I quickly adjusted to being solo for this ride. Weaknesses in this situation could get you killed!

I typed, "What's up?"

"Can we talk? Face-to-face. I just need to see you, to clear a few things up," she whined.

I sighed, feeling my frustration building.

"Yeah, meet me at the restaurant in an hour. I have a little free time," I said, shooting her the address.

When she arrived, I had the seating attendant walk her to the rear of the restaurant. I watched as she entered, then was seated. Her hair was longer now, softly brushing against her shoulders. A few faint lines formed around her eyes. Wearing that same beautiful smile that had me wrapped around her finger, giving her anything she asked for.

"Hey," I said, not wanting to startle her. "What's good?"

Vanessa's expression softened.

"Hi, Robert. It's... really good to see you."

She moved to embrace me, but I remained standing where I was. Vanessa released a deep sigh before taking her seat again, her fingers tapping softly on the stem of her wine glass.

"I didn't only ask you here to catch up," she admitted, her voice edged with tension. "I've got something I'd like to put out there."

"Okay. I'm listening."

"I've been replaying everything in my head, us—you know, what we had." She started. "And I messed that up because I was scared. I didn't know if I could hold you down for that long. So, leaving is what I knew how to do best. I want to get back to what we had." She paused. "I know there's still something between us."

Her words hung thick. With all the history we shared, never in a million years did I see it turning out like this. I thought she was my forever. Turned out, she was like every other woman I turned down for her ass. Selfish, greedy, and materialistic!

"Trust isn't a thing you just patch up once it's been violated. You shattered that shit!" I said, ironically calm. "When it's over, that shit is dead. Done!"

She stared at me with regret plastered over her face.

"Look, I get it, but I didn't want to leave anything between us unsaid."

"Cool," I said nonchalantly. "I met somebody and it's actually going pretty good. I'm not trying to have you interfere with that. I need you to let the past sit where it's at. Find somebody you can flow with. Love don't live here anymore." I chuckled.

"You met somebody, already?" Looking like she was trying to process what I had just said.

"Listen, I have some things I need to finish up in the office. Catch you another time," I said, standing to my feet, ending whatever this was.

"Robert, please!" she pleaded, sounding defeated.

"Be easy," I said, tossing the words over my shoulder, heading towards the elevator.

18

———

ON THE SAME TEAM

As I entered the house, there was an unsettling silence that greeted me. I placed my keys in the bowl on the mantel and headed upstairs; my body was craving a hot bath. After I adjusted the water to the perfect temperature, I eased myself into the tub, letting the heat seep into my aching muscles.

While my body began to relax, my mind was restless. Thoughts swirled through my head, grappling with how to repair my relationship. I often wondered if sharing my past would change the way Mario saw me.

A glance at the clock told me it was past eleven; Mario still hadn't come home.

I finished my bath and slipped into pajamas. Each passing minute, I accepted the fact that Mario may not come home tonight.

It was after midnight when he walked through the doors. When he entered the bedroom, he found me curled up on his side of the bed. He leaned over and gently kissed my shoulder.

I released a sleepy groan.

"Hey, you," he said, sitting next to me, slipping an arm around my waist. "You're still in your pajamas. Are you upset with me?"

"No. I'll change in a minute," I said, my voice drenched with exhaustion.

I could feel his breath on my neck. I loved that his presence always kept me rooted. Turning to face him, I kissed him so passionately; this was a rare moment of vulnerability for me. The way he held me felt so right. Natural. It was a feeling I was slowly getting used to, and I wanted it—with him.

Mario pulled me close, lifting me into his arms, my legs wrapping around his waist. I clung to him, covering his mouth with mine. His moan sparked something deep inside me. Our bodies moved in sync, moans filling the room like music.

That night, I made love for the very first time.

I loved him. I love his patience, his touch, the way he embraced every broken piece of me.

"There's something about you, Ms. Latoya," he whispered between kisses. "Something that keeps me intrigued with you."

I smiled, cradling his now-exhausted body against mine.

Sex with Mario was more than just physical. It was the attention, the intimacy, the way he made me feel. With him, I could be myself—flawed, real, whole.

"I never had a serious relationship before. I mean, I tried," I confessed. "I dated a few times, but it never worked out. I don't even know if I ever gave it a fair chance."

"Do you think you're giving us a fair chance?" he asked.

He looked at me so intently. I looked away. "I want to. I think I am. But how do I know you won't get tired of me... or change?"

"Because I've been the same man since day one," he said, pecking my lips. "And because I told you I wouldn't. If you've ever learned anything about me, then you should have learned that I always keep my word," he said, tapping my nose.

"I love you," I whispered.

Mario pulled back slightly, locking eyes with mine.

"You love me, baby?" he whispered.

I tried pulling away. It was already hard to say those words.

"Wait, hold up. Give a nigga a second. I've been waiting to hear you say those words, Ma!" He smiled before kissing me softly. "I love you, Ms. Latoya Marie Beaumont. A lot."

Tears brimmed my eyes as I clung to him, resting my head against his chest.

"Mario, there's still a lot you don't know about me."

"Like what? Talk to me," he said, kissing my forehead.

I turned toward him, lowering my eyes.

"When I was thirteen, my grandmother took me and my sister in to live with her. My mother used to leave us alone for days on end. Without food or heat in the winter. We didn't have water to even take a bath. I didn't find out until we left that she was addicted to heroin."

Mario remained quiet, his arm wrapped around me, his fingers tracing the outline of my body.

I turned my face from him.

"Look, just leave now. They always do. Why would you love somebody like me? There's too much—"

He cut me off, gently hooking my chin.

"You're a good woman, Latoya, and I love you just the way you are. Look, we both have scars, and I'm cool with that. I can handle that."

He kissed me so deeply, showing he meant every word.

"Mario, you don't understand just how damaged I am."

"Baby, we're all damaged! We're all fighting something. Don't shut me out—please give me the opportunity to love you right."

19

CRACKS IN THE FOUNDATION

Chloe was at home, music blasting as she powered through the spring-cleaning she'd been putting off for weeks. Mary J. Blige was her soundtrack, but no amount of scrubbing could keep her mind from drifting back to him.

When his name lit up her screen, her stomach flipped.

"Hey!" she answered, her excitement impossible to hide.

"Hey, gorgeous! Sounds like you're over there jammin'," I teased.

"Mary J. vibes all day," she laughed, twirling a loose strand of hair as she leaned against the counter.

"I was wondering if you'd like to come over for dinner. If it feels like it's too soon, I totally get it."

She blushed, her cheeks instantly turning red.

"I'd love to," she said, smiling. "Wait—can you even cook?"

"I'm no chef, but trust me, I know my way around a kitchen. You won't be disappointed," I chuckled.

Vanessa had been part of my life since college. We had big dreams and empty pockets. I gave her the life she wanted, and for a while, we were that couple everyone envied. But ambition can turn sour. She started getting greedy, ungrateful, taking me for granted. When I caught her cursing out Margie, I deaded that shit immediately. I told her if I saw that shit happen again, her ass was done. I loved her, so I tried to make it work, even when my brothers warned me to cut her ass off.

I walked into the kitchen, where Margie was slicing fruit.

"Hey," she said without looking up.

"Hey," I replied.

"What's on your mind?" she asked, still focused on the chopping board.

I told her about Chloe and the dinner invite. That made her pause—knife mid-air.

"Really? I'm happy for you, Robert. You deserve some happiness," she said, smiling.

I nodded, but my thoughts lingered.

"Vanessa texted the other day. Wanted to meet up, talk about getting back together."

Margie's head snapped toward me. "And you told her what? Please don't say you agreed. That girl nearly drove you crazy!"

I placed a hand on her shoulder, letting her know I understood where she was coming from. Margie had been loyal since day one. When the bust happened, my parents kept her on payroll so she wouldn't lose everything on my behalf. That loyalty earned her a permanent spot with us.

"I told her I've moved on. There's no place for her in my life," I said, grabbing a slice of fruit.

"Good. That's good," she said, sounding relieved. "I'll make a nice seafood platter for you and your new friend." By the upbeat of her voice, I could tell she was genuinely happy for me.

"Thanks, Margie," I said as I made my way to my office to make a few calls.

20

SECRETS AND SURVEILLANCE

Latoya sat on the edge of the bed, her hands fidgeting with the frayed seam of her sweater. The last bit of daylight spilled softly into the room, but the space between us felt thick—almost suffocating with all the things neither of us had said yet.

Just a few hours ago, what started as a small misunderstanding blew up into a full-blown fight. Voices got louder, frustration built up, and now there was an uncomfortable silence—the kind that comes after you say things you wished you hadn't.

Downstairs, I stood leaning against the kitchen door, staring out at the moonlit yard. My reflection in the window showed tired eyes, a face weighed down by regret. I couldn't stop replaying our argument, wishing I could take back those words. Latoya meant the world to me, and I knew I couldn't let us go to bed like this.

I made my way up to the bedroom, pausing at the door to pull myself together. I knocked quietly and stepped inside.

Latoya looked up, her eyes still red from holding back tears. I walked over, guilt written all over my face. She tried to hide how hurt she felt, but I knew her too well.

"Toya," I said in a gentle voice, "today's been rough for the both of us. I'm sorry about everything."

She held my gaze.

"I'm sorry too. I never wanted things to get this bad."

I sat down next to her, feeling drained. "I should've listened more. I let my stress do the talking instead of my heart."

Latoya leaned on me, her head resting softly against my back. "And I could've been more patient. I hate when we get so caught up in the heat of the moment."

We let the quietness hang between us, each of us thinking about what had just happened. But this time, the silence felt different—like we were finally on the same page.

I smiled at her, letting her know I meant what I had said. "Latoya, I love you. For real. You matter to me more than anything in this world."

She squeezed my hand, her smile slowly coming back. "I love you too. We're not perfect, but I believe in us. As long as we're honest with each other, I think we'll be okay."

I kissed her forehead and chuckled. "I'm still figuring out how to do this relationship thing."

The tension faded, and a comfortable calm replaced it. I glanced around the room, trying to lighten the mood. "How about we finally watch that movie we keep talking about?"

Latoya's eyes sparkled. "Love Jones? You already know that's my favorite!"

I kissed her passionately before preparing to set up the movie. "I can't stand going to bed mad."

She laughed, a real laugh this time. "Me neither. No more arguments before we go to bed."

Trust didn't come easy for her, especially when it came to relationships. But with every small moment like this, I was showing her that real love means working together through the tough times.

21

___

BLOOD BEFORE BUSINESS

Chloe and her girls settled in for one of their all-time favorite rituals—a cozy night of romance flicks, plenty of wine, and sharing stories that made them laugh, cringe, and sometimes tear up. I found myself curled up on Chloe's freshly redecorated sofa, absently circling the edge of my wine glass as my friends gathered around. Chloe sat nearby, draped over her chair with a laid-back vibe. Trudy had claimed a spot on the rug, clutching a pillow like it was her security blanket. Mousey squeezed herself into a corner of the couch, knees tucked close to her chest as she listened in.

The night started out just like any other—full of jokes, laughter, and silly conversations. But things quieted when I let out a heavy sigh, surprising myself with a sudden wave of reflection.

"Do you ever wonder how much your past makes you who you are?" I asked; my voice was a little softer than I intended.

Chloe perked up, curiosity in her eyes. "Oh, for sure. It's like we're all built from our past experiences."

Trudy nodded. "Yeah. Every little thing adds up, whether we realize it or not."

Mousey leaned forward, her expression gentle. "What made you come up with that, Latoya?"

I hesitated, swirling my wine before I responded. It wasn't my plan to get deep tonight, but I was feeling safe with my girls. I focused on the candle flickering on the coffee table, then found the words.

"There's something I rarely talk about," I admitted, voice barely above a whisper. "But I feel like maybe tonight's the night to talk about it."

Chloe straightened; all attention was on me. "We can definitely talk about it."

I glanced around at their faces, searching for reassurance. "Most of y'all know I had a tough childhood. Pam wasn't really around for me or Lydia. She struggled with addiction, and we bounced from pillar to post. I think you saw some of that over time."

Trudy's eyes softened. "Yeah, I remember hearing bits and pieces."

I managed a smile. "What got me through were the little things. Mostly Lydia. Grandma Louise always said I had a light inside me, something that couldn't go out—no matter how bad things got." I let out a quiet laugh, remembering her words.

Mousey's brow furrowed with concern. "So, what happened after high school?"

I glanced away, recalling those early years. "Grandma Louise scraped together enough for me to start college. I juggled jobs, classes, and eventually got a scholarship. But those first months? I was lost. Learning to budget with next to nothing was hard."

Chloe's expression was warm and proud. "You've come so far."

I placed my hands in my lap, feeling a wave of gratitude. "Having friends like you—all of you—who cared enough to stick around, it means the world. My past doesn't define me, but it definitely shaped my journey."

I paused, then quietly went on. "There's more... stuff I've kept hidden, like dealing with abuse from a lot of Pam's boyfriends—the beatings and the touches, all so they would leave Lydia alone."

The room went silent. The movie playing in the background faded. Suddenly it clicked for them—my guardedness, my mood swings—it all made sense.

Trudy reached across and gently squeezed my hand. "Thank you for trusting us, and I'm sorry that happened to you."

Mousey's voice wavered. "You've been through a lot, and you're still here."

I blinked rapidly, forcing back the tears that burned at the corners of my eyes. "Thanks. I didn't realize how much lighter I'd feel just letting it out."

Chloe leaned in with a reassuring smile. "You don't have to shoulder this pain alone, you know."

Mousey took my hands. "Please call me. We can talk about anything! You know I went through a lot of the same things you did."

I smiled, feeling the weight of my past lift from me. "I will call you, I promise." My lips curled into a genuine smile, and I mouthed back, "Thank you. I love y'all."

In that moment, I felt free. No longer bound by my secrets, the mood in the room softened. Our talk drifted to lighter things, and I realized we were more than friends—we were a family that we chose for ourselves.

As the night wore on and our laughter gave way to gentle quiet, Chloe caught the flicker of pain still shadowing my eyes. She scooted closer and spoke gently. "Latoya, look, I know a therapist—someone I trust who's helped women through some dark times. I'm here for you through every step of your therapy if you decide to see her. You're my best friend, and I love you."

Our eyes met, and I nodded, feeling vulnerable but understood. "I know. It's just... I didn't know where to start."

We hugged—one of those long, safe embraces that said everything words couldn't. In that moment, it wasn't just about friendship. It was true sisterhood.

22

———

THE MAN WE BURIED

I pulled up to Robert's house right as the last rays of sunlight painted everything gold. I couldn't help but stare—the place looked straight out of a movie. His house, three floors tall with ivy trailing down the sides, had that perfect balance of old-school charm and modern vibes. It sat on a huge, open lot with no neighbors crowding in, which made it feel extra peaceful. Despite how big the place was, I instantly felt at ease because it totally fit Robert's laid-back style.

Before I could even knock, the front door swung open. Robert stood there grinning, his dark locs pulled back, looking effortlessly cool in a shirt that somehow managed to be both casual and sharp. "Hey, Miss Chloe. Wow, you look incredible," he said, his eyes shining with genuine appreciation.

I laughed, cheeks warming as I stepped inside. The whole house smelled incredible—herbs and spices floated in the air, making my stomach rumble. "I'm starving. What'd you cook?" I asked, curiosity in my voice.

"Come see for yourself," Robert said, nodding toward the kitchen.

The kitchen could've been lifted from a home décor magazine: neat but inviting, shiny pots hanging above a spotless stove, and a rich mahogany table set for just the two of them. Soft under-cabinet lights made everything feel cozy and chilled.

"It smells delicious," I said, taking a deep breath.

Robert grinned. "Lobster tails, shrimp scampi, scallops with asparagus. Family recipes, kind of." He shot me a playful smirk.

"I raised a skeptical eyebrow. "You're telling me you cooked all this yourself?"

He laughed. "Okay, maybe not all by myself. But I wanted tonight to be special for you—to give you a night you'd remember."

We sat down at the table, raising our glasses to toast to new beginnings and lifelong friendships. The conversation flowed, laughter echoing between us, and I felt a sense of peace I hadn't experienced in ages.

What struck me the most was how present he was. He didn't just listen; he was tuned in like I was the only person in the world. Dinner was incredible, but the company was even better.

"That was amazing," I said, leaning back, totally satisfied.

"Glad you liked it," Robert replied. "Honestly, someone special came through with the food. It's been a while since I've had good company."

"I might need to get Miss Margie's recipes for myself," I giggled.

"Only if you promise to join me for dinner again," he teased.

"I think we can make that happen," I said, my voice teasing him right back.

As darkness fell and candles flickered, the room's energy shifted— deeper, more intimate. Robert reached across the table, his fingers brushing across my face. I looked up, my breath catching as our eyes met.

"Chloe," he said softly, "there's something I've been meaning to tell you..."

He leaned in, closing the space between us with a gentle kiss. It was deliberate, sweet, with a whole lot of meaning.

"Thank you," I whispered, barely audible.

"For what?" he asked, wrapping me in a gentle embrace.

Our eyes stayed locked, the air charged between us. Robert cradled my face, his thumb tracing my cheek.

"I'm really glad you came," he said quietly.

"Me too," I replied, my voice just above a breath.

The night carried on, full of laughter and easy conversation. Nothing forced—just two people finding their groove in one another.

Later, stepping into the cool night air, I felt something new stirring inside. That kiss wasn't just a kiss. It felt like a promise.

Smiling to myself, I realized I was genuinely happy.

23

———

RESURRECTION

I sat on the couch, staring at my phone, my mind filled with doubt. Therapy? Was that really for me? Pam's voice replayed in my head: "How somebody gone tell you, a perfectly sound-minded person, how to change? If you don't want to change, you won't!" Those words stung. But then Chloe's voice cut through the noise, softer but stronger: "Asking for help isn't weakness. It's strength. I'm so proud of you!"

With a heavy sigh, I picked up my phone. My heart thudded hard as I dialed the number Chloe had given me. This was something I had to do for me. I wasn't ready for Mario to know until I had things figured out. I needed time. I was finally taking control of my mental health.

The waiting room was quiet. I sat near the door, fidgeting with the hem of my sweater. The ticking of the clock on the wall made every second feel heavier.

Then the door opened. A woman in her late forties stepped out, her smile warm, her eyes kind.

"Latoya?" she asked gently.

I stood, straightening my posture, and followed the assistant into a softly lit room that smelled like lavender.

"I'm Dr. Mendez," the therapist said, motioning to a chair across from her.

I sat, my breath shallow, silence lingering between us.

"So, Latoya," Dr. Mendez began, "what brings you in today?"

My voice barely rose above a whisper. "I... I guess I've been feeling overwhelmed. I'm tired of carrying the weight of my past."

Dr. Mendez nodded, her expression calm and open. "Would you like to tell me more about what that looks like for you?"

I hesitated, eyes dropping to the rug. "It's Pam," I said nonchalantly. "She's been addicted to drugs for as long as I can remember. I had to raise my little sister, Lydia, since I was seven. It forced me to grow up fast."

"Pam?" Dr. Mendez asked softly.

"My mother," I clarified. "She didn't like me calling her 'Mama.' I stopped around four."

Dr. Mendez's pen moved quietly across her notepad. "Four is so young to take on that kind of responsibility. What was that like for you?"

I exhaled slowly, memories spilling out like worn pages. "I'd come home from school and never know what I'd find. Sometimes she'd be there. Sometimes gone for days. By the age of six, I had to cook, clean, change Lydia's diapers. I was just a kid—trying to be a mom when I barely knew how to care for myself."

Dr. Mendez met my eyes, allowing me to feel safe. For the first time, I felt something loosen inside, like a knot coming undone.

"It was hard," I said; my voice was calmer now. "I missed out on being a kid. I only had one friend who ever came over. I was afraid someone would find out how bad it was. All I wanted was to protect Lydia."

"Did anyone support you back then?" Dr. Mendez asked.

I shook my head. "No. I felt alone. At school, I'd smile like everything was fine. But inside? I was terrified."

Dr. Mendez nodded slowly. "And now?"

I thought of Mario—how he'd walked into my life like a hero. "I met someone. Mario. He makes me feel... loved. He treats me like I matter."

"What does that feel like for you?" Dr. Mendez asked.

"It feels... foreign," I admitted, my brow softening. "He listens. He laughs with me. It's like he sees me. But sometimes I wonder if it's real. I'm always bracing for when he changes."

Dr. Mendez leaned in slightly. "It's understandable to feel that way when so much of your life has been uncertain. Mario sounds like a positive presence in your life. How does being with him change how you see yourself?"

I paused. "I'm still learning. Sometimes I think, maybe I do deserve this. Other times, I don't believe I deserve any of it. After everything with Pam... I keep waiting for the other shoe to drop."

"That's valid," Dr. Mendez said gently. "Your caution is a form of protection. But just being here today shows you're starting to believe you deserve something better."

I felt something warm stir in my chest.

"I want more for Lydia. For myself. I want to break the cycle."

Dr. Mendez smiled. "That's a powerful goal. And you're already on that path. Therapy isn't about fixing what's broken, Latoya—it's about reclaiming your strength. Finding your voice and trusting that you're worthy of peace and happiness."

I nodded slowly, afraid of what to expect moving forward. "I just want to be okay."

Dr. Mendez's smile deepened. "That's a beautiful place to start."

As the session went on, I shared more of the truths I had buried for years. Each word felt lighter on my shoulders. And when I stepped back into my life, I held on to something unfamiliar yet real:

Hope.

Maybe, just maybe, I could give Mario the love he deserved. Because now, I was starting to believe I deserved it too.

24

WHAT REVENGE COSTS

A few weeks later, the vibe at my place was just right. Cozy and laid-back. Perfect setup for tonight's get-together. Chloe had been counting the days until this dinner, eager to finally meet the people who meant so much to me. I wanted her to see me in my element so she could get to really know me.

As she parked and walked up to the door, she felt a rush of nerves and excitement hitting her all at once. I opened the door with a huge grin, greeting her like I hadn't seen her in years and pulling her into me.

"Hey, beautiful! You made it. Everyone's here," I said, whispering close to her ear.

She grinned, feeling instantly more at ease. "Thank you. Honestly, I've been looking forward to meeting your friends."

I shook my head and smiled. "Friends? Baby, they're my people."

Inside, the living room was buzzing. Mario and Mookie were posted up on the couch, each with their own vibe. Mario was just as tall as I was, with Mookie just a tad bit shorter than the both of us. Mookie was the one who was always full of energy, and between the three of us, he was known as the life of the party. The jokester, but he wasn't the one to be messed with when it came to putting in work. None of us were.

"Chloe, meet my brothers, Mario and Mookie," I announced, motioning to the duo. "Mario's the more serious of the two; Mookie's the life of the party."

Mario stood, offering his hand with a smile. "Hi, Chloe. Nice to finally meet you. Robert talks about you all the time," he said, a teasing glint in his eye.

"Nice to meet you too," Chloe replied, accepting the friendly embrace.

Mookie popped up next, all energy. "Yo, Chloe! I'm Mookie. The way my brother has been hyping you up, I already know you're cool people," he said, winking and giving her a warm embrace.

Chloe laughed, feeling a bit more relaxed. "Thank you, Mookie. I think we're gonna get along just fine."

Suddenly, the doorbell rang. My grin got even bigger as I looked toward the foyer. "Stoney, your girl's here!" I called out.

Chloe perked up, recognizing the voice at the door. She hurried over, eyes wide. "Latoya? I'm glad you came!"

"Girl!" Latoya squealed, hugging and swaying as they laughed.

I stared, surprised. I told her to bring her girls, but I didn't know it was Mario's girl.

"Wait, you two know each other?"

Mookie played up the moment, pretending to be shocked. "No way! Chloe knows Latoya? This is crazy!"

I shook my head, laughing, while they were too caught up to notice.

"Mario, did you know they were friends?" I asked as he joined them, greeting Latoya with a kiss. In that moment, something clicked—like the universe had lined things up perfectly, bringing all these connections together.

Back in the living room, laughter and stories flew around. Mario shared wild college stories, while Mookie animatedly talked about losing a big-time basketball game because of a missed layup.

When I stepped out to take a call, Chloe took the opportunity to chat with Mario and Mookie. "So, how did you all become so close?" she asked, sipping her drink. "You really seem like family."

Mario smiled. "We've been through everything. Robert moved near me when we were kids, and we just clicked. Been best friends ever since."

Mookie nodded. "Robert's a solid dude. You won't find anybody better than him. I promise you."

Chloe's smile grew. She couldn't argue with that. Mookie turned to Latoya. "What about you, Latoya? Do you have any family in the city?"

Latoya's smile faltered just a little. "No, not really. It's just me out here," she said softly, then asked, "Um, where's the bathroom?"

Sensing her discomfort, Mario jumped in gently. "Just past the foyer, to the right," he told her.

Latoya got up, smoothing her dress, and Mario followed close behind. In the hallway, he caught up with her, wrapping her in an embrace. Lifting her chin, he looked into her eyes and asked softly, "You okay?"

She nodded, voice barely above a whisper. "I'm fine. I just miss my family, that's all."

Mario smiled, reassuring. "I'll handle it. Make sure you see them soon," he promised, brushing a gentle kiss against her cheek.

Back in the living room, Chloe sat, taking it all in. Being with Robert's family made her feel closer to him.

"Glad you're having a good time," I said. "I wanted you to see this part of my life."

"I'm really glad I'm here," she replied.

I leaned in, kissing her. A simple moment that said everything.

As the evening wound down, Chloe and Latoya gathered their things, sharing one last look around the cozy living room. I caught Chloe's eye and tapped my ear, mouthing, "Call me." She couldn't help but laugh, nodding she would. Across the room, Mario mouthed to Latoya, "See you when I get home, love. I'll be leaving soon." Latoya gave him a gentle smile with love in her eyes.

Stepping outside together, Chloe and Latoya linked arms, their laughter carrying into the quietness. They walked down the porch steps, smiles lingering, wrapped in that easy sense of belonging you only find when you're with people who truly get you.

ACT III

COLLISION

25

THE NAME BEAUMONT

It was late afternoon and the sun was beginning to set. I sat on the edge of my sofa, my fingers tapping a restless rhythm against the armrest. My eyes kept darting to the clock—five glances in four minutes, not that I was counting. Chloe was supposed to show up any second now.

It had only been a few days since we last hung out; it just felt so long. There was something about this woman. Her smile. The way it could change my mood in seconds, and the way she did that shy little gesture where she'd cover her mouth when she laughed. But what really hit differently was her energy. Chloe was a kind and gentle soul, and her energy was always positive. She was the opposite of the women I was used to dating.

Vanessa came to mind. In the beginning, meeting her felt like finding a diamond in the rough. She was so down-to-earth and grateful for everything. As my pockets got deeper, her appetite grew.

I shook off the bitter throwback. Right on cue, the doorbell broke the silence, bringing me back to reality. I straightened my shirt, brushed the imaginary lint from my sleeve, and headed to the door.

There she was, just as I imagined—her smile bright and calming, her hands casually resting in the pockets of her jeans.

"Hey," she greeted warmly, stepping inside.

My face softened, something that seemed to come naturally since she had entered my life. I brought her close to me. Her perfume consumed me. It was like a spell she had me under. I pulled back and led her from the entryway into the living room.

"Would you like something to drink?" I asked.

Chloe shook her head, the edges of her smile hesitating slightly. "No, thank you," she said, a hint of apprehension threading through her words. "You said you needed to talk, so I came right over."

"Yeah, nothing too serious. I just wanted to run something by you, that's all."

Her shoulders relaxed; a softer expression covered her face.

"Okay," she said, perching on the loveseat near the foyer.

I chuckled, taking her hand, tugging her gently toward the lounge area.

"Come on, don't make it seem so serious," I teased.

She raised an eyebrow, her comeback as quick as mine.

"Oh? Then why call me over instead of just telling me over the phone?"

Before I could respond, the sound of footsteps interrupted our conversation. Ms. Walker, my housekeeper, appeared in the doorway.

"Mr. Allen, do you or your guest need anything before I go?" she asked.

I gazed in her direction.

"No, thank you, Ms. Walker. If we need anything, I'll handle it."

She gave a courteous nod before going back into the house.

"Have a good night."

As her footsteps faded, Chloe turned back to me, her curiosity piqued.

"So, what's up?"

"Let's just say this is a conversation that needed to happen."

Once Ms. Walker was gone, I shifted my attention back to Chloe, my tone dropping into something more intimate.

"So... there are a few things I think you need to hear from me."

Chloe straightened in her seat; her attention focused on what I was about to say.

"Like what things?" she asked.

I cleared my throat.

"My ex—Vanessa came to see me last week."

Chloe raised her brows slightly. "Vanessa? You barely talk about her. What did she want?"

"She reached out to me thinking we could get back together. She talking about she's looking for closure."

Chloe leaned in, not sure how she should feel.

"What did you think about her suggestion?"

I exhaled slowly, my eyes shifting away, then back to Chloe.

"Honestly, I felt torn. Part of me wanted to hear her out, to understand her side. But another part told me not to give it the time of day."

Chloe's expression softened, her tone steady.

"What actually happened between you two?"

"It started unraveling when I was upstate, serving my time. I had a hard time reaching Vanessa for weeks. Every time I called, it went straight to voicemail. Days turned into weeks and weeks turned into months, still nothing. I finally reached out to my brother, Ant, because I couldn't take not knowing. It was a hard pill to swallow. She didn't really love me. She loved the things I could do for her."

Chloe tilted her head slightly, her eyes steady as she listened to my story.

I told her about the night Ant crossed paths with her best friend, Peaches, and she shared what Vanessa was doing whenever I called.

Chloe let out a soft chuckle, shaking her head in disbelief.

"I wasn't useful anymore because she thought I couldn't give her all the things she wanted because of the circumstances."

Chloe's eyebrows shot up, her face twisted in shock. "Wow, that's messed up!"

I tossed my glass of cognac back, remembering the pain and disappointment.

"And then she pops up over here acting like we had a chance to fix that shit.

Once I shut a door, that muthafucka is locked."

Sitting to face Chloe, my expression turned serious.

"Trust and loyalty are everything to me," I said quietly. "Once that's broken... there's nothing left."

Her gaze held mine. "I understand," she muttered.

I was feeling the weight of the moment, the undeniable pull of my feelings for her. Chloe had a way of disarming me, bringing out a vulnerability I never expected. I knew I couldn't afford to slip up. I didn't want to.

"I need you to know that Vanessa is the past and she will not come between us," I told her. "What we have—it's real, and I want to see where this goes."

Chloe grabbed my hand; her touch was grounding me, and she didn't even know it. "Robert, you've been upfront with me since we first met, and so I trust you. I'm here and I'm not going anywhere."

I met her gaze and saw it. Her loyalty was unwavering and pure.

"Transparency means a lot to me. If there's doubt... it's not worth having because there's no trust."

Chloe's fingers tightened gently around mine.

"And as far as Vanessa is concerned, if you need to see her again to set things straight, do whatever you have to do. I trust you."

My lips curved into a smile. The tension faded from my muscles.

"I got it, Ma. I'm glad we can talk about it."

26

———

SNAKE IN THE ROOM

We'd been hyping this night up for weeks. Finally, it was here. Everyone claimed their usual spots, bowls of popcorn and snacks within reach, wine glasses in hand.

I dimmed the lights just right and grinned. "Alright, ladies—tonight is all about us. No adulting, no rules. Just laughs, stories, and girl time!"

Latoya, mid-bite into a cookie, threw her hands up. "Yes! I've been waiting for this. And trust me, I've got some stuff."

Mousey leaned in with a big smile. "Same here. I've got some hilarious work stories."

Trudy was already eyeing the nail polish lineup. "Perfect. But first—Truth or Dare?"

The room erupted in giggles. Latoya went first, choosing "Truth" with a mischievous grin. "Okay, Chloe. What's one thing you've never told anyone?"

I froze. My cheeks were hot, turning red. After I took a deep breath, I said, "Alright... this is big. I think I'm in love. I haven't told a soul—until now."

Mousey's jaw dropped. "Stop! Chloe, what! Finally!"

I croaked out a laugh, looking around at my girls.

"I know, right? It just happened... and I think I'm ready."

"I knew it!" Latoya squealed, clapping her hands and bouncing in her seat. "Y'all are so cute!"

My girls were genuinely happy for me. It had been years since David, and I deserved someone who would put my happiness first.

Trudy leaned toward Mousey. "Your turn. Truth or dare?"

Mousey chewed her lip. "Truth."

Trudy smirked. "What's the most embarrassing thing that's ever happened to you?"

Mousey groaned. "Okay, this is bad. Went on a date, got way too drunk, and threw up in his car. Girl, he ghosted me so hard and never answered a single call from me since!"

The room exploded with laughter, Mousey laughing too now that the shame had faded.

I patted her back. "We've all got one of those kinds of stories."

Trudy grabbed a bottle of purple polish. "Alright, who's first for nails?"

Latoya shot her a death stare.

"Last time you painted mine, I ended up with polish all over my good jeans!"

As Trudy worked on Latoya's nails, Chloe and Mousey reached for more chips.

"So," I said, "tell me about this new job."

Mousey grinned. "I'm officially a Social Worker with Children's Services!"

Latoya looked up, impressed. "Wow! That's great, Sis! That education paid off for you!"

Mousey nodded. "Thank you, Sis. You know my story. I didn't have it easy by a long shot. Foster care saved us."

Trudy chimed in, finishing Latoya's nails. "Speaking of life… Latoya, I heard you and Mario are solid now. No more drama!"

Latoya shot up. "Sorry to disappoint you by being happy," she snapped, rolling her eyes.

Trudy raised her hands. "Whoa, that's not what I meant. I'm happy for you! We all are."

Latoya spun around. "Happy because someone finally puts up with my shit, huh? Is that what you're trying to say?"

Trudy frowned. "Girl, no! Hell, I'm still looking for somebody who can handle my ass!"

Sensing the tension between my girls, I slipped out and came back with a bottle of bubbles, the kind you keep for the neighborhood kids. I blew streams of bubbles across the room.

"Come on, y'all. Tonight is supposed to be about fun!"

Mousey ducked, laughing. "Girl, if these bubbles mess up my hair, we're going to be fighting next!"

The laughter was back, and we continued the night like it was supposed to be—stories, secrets, and laughter. I shared my happiness with Robert. Latoya opened up about Mario and her fears of dating. Trudy admitted she dreamed of marriage and kids. Mousey spoke about her mom's addiction and the fight it took to raise her siblings.

We listened, loved, and lifted each other. By the time our conversations died down, there was nothing but soft snores filling the room. I laid there smiling. I was grateful for this sisterhood we built. We're friends forever.

27

THE MESSAGE

Mario's office was a mess. The mahogany table sitting in the center of the office was covered with stacks of paperwork—organized chaos. The blinds let in just enough light to throw stripes on the walls, shadows creeping in.

He leaned back in his chair, cracking his knuckles, before leaning forward again. This wasn't just another meeting.

Beans sat across from him, posted up like he owned shit. Wearing a clean Armani suit, a gun strap on his side, with two iced-out rings on his left hand that caught every bit of light in the room. His posture said he was ready if shit went sideways.

Mario was breaking down their next move on how they could reclaim the streets. The streets had been wild for a minute. The local niggas couldn't hold it down, and they were tired of cleaning up their mess.

"So, the drop's still good for tomorrow night?" he asked, his eyes locked on Beans.

He nodded; his face was tight. "Yeah. It's on. But..." He paused. "I've been hearing some noise—like somebody's trying to jack your spots. Looks like it's moving from the inside."

He sucked his teeth. "Fuck, don't tell me that shit when we're already bleeding for time. If somebody is moving grimy under my nose, they better pray I don't find 'em first."

Beans was just about to continue when the office door sprung open.

I casually walked in, nonchalant, until I noticed Beans.

I froze. Our eyes locked on each other.

My whole mood shifted and my eyes narrowed. Everything seemed to move in slow motion.

Mario's head whipped towards the door. "Yooo, what the—?"

"I'm sorry, baby, I didn't know you were in a meeting," my eyes fixated on Beans.

"Officer Brimley?" I muttered.

Beans's body tensed. He was unsure if his cover had been blown.

He glanced up, confused. "Hey, babe. You good?" His eyes bounced between us.

I shook my head, trying to steady myself as if I saw a ghost. "No, I'm good," I said quietly. Beans watched as I leaned in, pressing a quick kiss to Mario's lips before quickly leaving.

Mario sat in his La-Z-Boy positioned near the front door, his hand drumming steadily on the armrest as he tried to make sense of the situation from earlier. Once I entered the house, his eyes were fixated on me.

"Latoya," he called out, his voice calm.

"Hey. Why are you sitting in the dark?"

"How familiar are you with Beans?"

My heart pounded. He'd seen it—the way we recognized one another.

I drew in a shaky breath, then began sharing my story.

"Pam had been gone for days, like she had many times before. We ran out of food. My friend Keisha would share her dinner with us when she could. That whole week, she hadn't come over. Lydia was still a baby... and she had been crying for hours. We were hungry."

I paused, my throat tightening.

"I went through Pam's old clothes and found something that would make me appear older—sixteen, maybe."

My voice wavered, but I pressed on.

"I walked the streets for hours and I didn't make any money. A car pulled up with tinted windows and shiny rims, looking like money. He rolled down his window and offered me two hundred dollars."

Closing my eyes, I allowed the tears to fall as I recalled that night.

Mario remained quiet. As hard as it was, he had to hear the whole story.

I continued. "Two hundred felt like a million dollars at that moment. I told him I'd do whatever he wanted, but he had to give me the money first. He said he would, once I got in the car. I'd been robbed before; I knew better. But I was desperate. So, I got in."

Tears rimmed my eyes.

"As soon as I got in the car, he locked the doors and flashed a badge. My heart dropped. He said he was taking me to jail!" I sobbed uncontrollably. "I begged him to let me go. I told him I had to get my sister. He didn't buy it and drove me to the police station. Another police officer told him to take me home and grab Lydia before calling CPS. Beans—Officer Brimley—was the officer who arrested me. But he's also the person who saved our lives. Instead of calling CPS, he called

Grandma Louise. He went against orders just to help us. He didn't have to do any of that."

Mario's eyes softened. Suddenly he understood their connection. In his line of business, he didn't trust people easily.

"So yeah," I said, my voice cracking. "That's how I know him."

Tears slid down my face. I stood, my body trembling, unsure what to expect next. Mario stood with me, wrapping his arms around me. His face nestled into my neck.

"Baby, I'm sorry, but I had to know. Damn, baby, that took a lot of courage. And the way she left you and your sister... damn!" He muttered.

Hearing her story made him love her even more. It made him understand why she kept running.

But this news brought on new problems.

Beans was an undercover cop, and he had made it inside their circle.

I curled up on the bed facing the wall. Mario stepped in quietly and sat on the edge of the bed. He reached out and gently tapped my shoulder.

"Hey, are you awake?"

I rolled over to face him. My eyes were puffy and red with fresh tears.

"I'm sorry," I whispered. "I was going to tell you when you got home."

"There's no way you could've known who I was meeting with. That's on me. I got this. I should've noticed that something was off—look, this isn't something you need to worry about."

He leaned in, kissing my forehead.

"I'm going to step out for a minute; I need to handle a few things. I might be late getting back, but understand I'm coming home. You hear me? I'm always coming home."

Mario jumped in his car, snatching up his phone, his thumb tapping quickly on the keyboard. Money.

"Yo!" Robert answered lightly.

"Hey," Mario said. "I'm headed to your spot. Hit up Mookie and let him know to meet me there."

Robert didn't ask questions. His tone said it all.

Trouble was no longer knocking—it was already there, on the inside.

28

———

EVERYTHING COMES BACK

I was on edge after seeing Latoya walk into Mario's office. My posture shifted, spun into a tightening spiral possibly playing out worse than I could ever imagine.

"Fuck!" I muttered, my fingers clenching the steering wheel of my Mercedes-Maybach S 580.

I was a man who exhibited self-control, always predicting my every move. But now? My investigation was hanging by a thread. One wrong move, and it could all come crashing down.

I sat parked outside the house where I knew one of Latoya's friends lived.

I checked the rearview mirror. I was unshaven, dark circles formed beneath my eyes, a weight hanging from my shoulders not even sleep could fix. I needed a trim, a shower, and a week full of rest. But right now, none of that mattered.

Climbing the steps, I ran through every detail of my last run-in with Latoya. The flagged department logs, the unauthorized access from the files of information I had collected.

I knocked hard. The door creaked open to barely a crack. Her friend Chloe stood behind it, her eyes narrowing as she looked me over, suspiciously.

"I'm looking for Latoya," I said calmly, no drama. "I'm a friend."

She appeared behind Chloe in the doorway. Her eyes widened from shock, caught off guard, but she quickly recovered.

"Hey," she said, her voice warm with a tense undertone.

"We need to talk," I said, stepping inside.

She shut the door and turned to face me.

"I take it that this is no social call, huh?"

"Nah," I said, forcing a smile. "I need to know if you told Mario who I was?"

Her jaw tensed. "Why?" she shot back, before her voice softened. "Look... I don't lie to Mario. He's the first man who's ever loved me. And I love him too."

I took a slow, deliberate breath. "I'm not after Mario, but it's someone he knows."

"If it's not Mario, then who?" she asked.

She wasn't sure where the line was drawn between love and loyalty, feeling like she owed me a lot.

She dropped down onto the couch.

"Why can't you use somebody else? Somebody besides him to get close to whoever it is you're after?"

I shook my head.

"Now that Mario knows who I am, you're the only link I have. If he doesn't believe we're still working together, the whole case goes cold, and it's all wasted."

Her eyes fell, twisting her fingers nervously.

"Alright... but I'm only asking one thing, Mario won't get caught up in all of this. You can't put him in a spot where he's facing time. If you can't promise me that, then we're done talking. There's nothing else to say."

I ran a hand over my face.

"Alright. I'll do everything within my power that there's no jail time for Mario or his brothers."

She nodded, feeling better about the situation, although she still felt torn.

"I'll let you know what he decides to do. Please promise me this will be the last time we meet without Mario."

"My word," I said.

I turned to leave but instead, I hesitated.

"Latoya, for what it's worth, I'm glad you're okay. I thought a lot about you and your sister, hoping you both made it out." Offering a faint smile before stepping through the threshold.

Latoya collapsed into Chloe's arms. Her tears were streaming down her face. The past she thought was buried had found its way back into her life, and this time, it wasn't just her heart on the line.

29

———

THE CHRISTMAS THAT BROKE ME

I turned slowly toward the window, lost in a memory. My voice was low, dripping with hatred.

"I had a crack whore for a mother. You ever go to sleep with Christmas gifts under the tree, then wake up and everything—tree, presents, food, TV—gone? Every fucking thing—gone. We were so hungry that day, I hit the corner where the dope boys posted up. I told them I'd be the best drug runner they ever had. Two hours later, I had six hundred dollars in my pocket and a fridge full of food."

Beans leaned back, listening, trying to piece together who his partner truly was.

I kept going; my jaw was tight.

"First few months she got hooked, she'd sneak in and steal meat from the freezer—chicken, steak, salmon, whatever she could flip. Didn't matter that her kids were starving. I caught her once; I damn near beat her ass to death."

"I thought you were an orphan," Beans said carefully.

"We were," I replied flatly. "Pamela Cherise got so twisted on crack and heroin, she once mistook me for Gunna—some big-time dealer on her block. She came skipping around the corner, thinking she was going to trick for a hit. When she saw me, I told her to meet me behind the Chicken King at 7:30. Told her I had an eight ball for her."

I pinched the bridge of my nose as the picture became clear as day. My voice dropped to a growl.

"She showed up on time." I released a low chuckle. "I pulled my hood back. She saw my face. And you know what she did? I waved that eight ball in her face, and like the fiend she was, she was still ready to trick for it! Me. Her son," I said, stabbing my chest with my finger.

My voice cracked, then I exploded.

"So, I blessed her ass. One to the dome," I said, mimicking a gun at my temple before lowering my hand.

Stunned, Beans just stared at me.

"You iced your moms?" he whispered.

I lit a cigarette, the flame trembling just slightly. I inhaled, exhaled; I was calmer but felt hollow.

"She wasn't my mother anymore. She was a fiend."

The smoke swirled heavily in the silence.

* * *

A couple of days later, I stood in front of a picture-framed window with my jaw tight. My mind replayed the report I'd received from Base.

Vanessa, Money's girl, was spotted at the trap spot with Loco.

My voice had been calm, almost too calm.

"The trap spot, huh? Guess it's time to pay Vanessa a little visit."

I was lost in my thoughts. I barely noticed Beans watching me.

"So, what's on your mind? You been staring out that window for an hour," Beans joked, trying to lighten the mood.

"Not thinking on shit," I said, my eyes still fixated outside. Then, almost to myself, I whispered, "You ever been so close to your dreams it feels like you're already living that muthafucka?"

Beans chuckled, slumping back.

"Hell yeah. When I was seven, I was so hungry I'd watch another kid eat and felt like I could taste his food."

I turned around and stared at him, partly amused.

"That's how I got my nickname," Beans said with a half-smile, drifting back.

I smirked. "What was he eating, beans?"

"You wild," Beans laughed. "But yeah. I stole a can of pork and beans from the corner store. I didn't even wait. Used a pocketknife, cracked it open, ate 'em cold in the alley. Cops found me there, face buried in the can. Word spread around the neighborhood and from then on, I was known as the Pork and Bean kid from the Pork and Beans projects."

I blinked, surprised. In all the years I'd worked with Beans, I had never heard that story.

30

NO ONE TELLS HER YET

Everyone was gathered in my office. I sat behind the mahogany desk. Mookie released a low whistle. "All the intelligence we have at our fingertips, how the hell we missed this nigga?"

"How? Why? You've been moving under our noses for months—what's up with that?" Robert asked, his chest tight.

"The fact that he's even sitting here right now says everything! I think we need to hear what he has to say," I suggested.

"Hear him out?" Robert asked with a low chuckle that sounded more like a growl.

"Yes, hear the man out!" I said sternly.

"Okay, what is it that you want to say?" Robert asked in a sarcastic tone.

Beans calmly sat waiting to speak, as if he hadn't just told us he was an undercover cop.

"My partner came to me about a year ago," Beans started. "He said we had been reassigned to keep tabs on a restaurant owner and his crew.

Claimed they were involved with transporting for the cartels. I had no reason to doubt him. Six months later, Internal Affairs showed up at my doorstep, revealing they were investigating him."

Robert released a sharp breath. "Let me guess—their investigation involved us too."

"Not exactly," Beans replied. "They were more interested in why he was looking into you and your company, and whether the information he collected could be verified. That's when shit started to fall in place—he was dirty. Taking hushed calls and disappearing mid-shift. Shit just wasn't adding up."

Mookie shifted his posture. "So, I'm curious to know what information you have so far. Is there something we should be concerned about?"

"Nah, nothing. The department has concluded that my partner was chasing a ghost. Here's the kicker, though—he's been working with Tae'Quan LeZander."

Our heads snapped toward Beans.

"Zander?" they echoed in unison.

"What does Zander have to do with us?" Robert asked, his brows furrowed. "We haven't seen or spoken with him in years since our release."

Beans laid out everything he'd uncovered, saving one final revelation for last. He recounted a conversation he'd had with New York, in which New York shared how he had killed his mother, Pamela Charise Beaumont, a few years earlier. My expression shifted; I was definitely caught off guard by that.

"Beaumont?" I asked. I needed to confirm what I had just heard.

"Latoya's last name is Beaumont, and she told me her mother's name was Pam. Said she hadn't heard from her in a while."

Mookie and Robert appeared shocked. I regained my composure and came up with a plan to track Zander down. I needed to somehow share with Latoya the information Beans had just shared with us.

"No one is to say a word to Latoya. I'll decide when and how she's told," I said.

Robert clapped my back.

"You good?"

"Nah, but I will be."

31

SISTERS AND GHOSTS

I sat on the edge of my bed, clutching my phone tight, staring at the screen. The walls around me felt like they were closing in. My thumb hovered over my sister's name, but it had been months since I'd reached out.

Every time I thought about calling, my stomach twisted with guilt and grief, all tangled up.

I finally hit the call button.

Three rings before Lydia's voice sounded through the phone.

"Hello?"

"Hey... it's me," I whispered.

There was a long pause before Lydia's voice broke the silence.

"Latoya?" Lydia finally said, voice breaking. She missed me so much. She was the only family I had left since Grandma Louise passed away.

"I know," I said, voice low. "I just... wanted to hear your voice."

"How have you been?" Lydia asked, with worry in her voice.

"I'm okay. Just keeping busy," I said, leaning back against the headboard, my breath shaky. "But it's been hard lately not hearing from Pam."

"Yeah," Lydia nodded. "For me too."

Another pause between them.

"I know I shouldn't," my voice cracked, "but... I miss her."

"I miss her too," Lydia whispered back.

Pam had broken us. Shattered our childhood and left us stretched and frayed by her drug abuse.

I shut my eyes. The memory replayed clearly in my head.

The door slamming.

Pam's voice, impatient and brash: "Naw naw, Toya, don't cry. I'll be back, damn! Okay... okay, look, I'll bring you a doll!"

Nine-year-old me stood blocking the door with my small frame, desperate. Pam shifted, fidgeting. "You don't want a doll? Okay, look, shit! I'll be back! Now move!"

Grandma Louise gently stepped in. Her hands tugged my shoulders.

"Come on, baby, let's make that cake you and Lydia like so much," she coaxed.

But I shook my head, sobbing harder than I had the first time Pam left.

"I don't want that cake no more! Why can't I go with her, Grandma Louise?"

We both knew, deep down, Pam wasn't coming back.

As time went on, it had been so long that nobody ever bothered to wait for her to return. When she finally rolled through again, Lydia and I no longer referred to her as Mama. She was just Pam.

"Keep calling me Pam and see what happens!" she barked, her voice hoarse, quivering from years of drug abuse. Her clothes were filthy. Her skin, ashy and hollow. She didn't even smell like a person anymore.

I stood firm.

"What do you want me to call you, Pam?" My tone was sharp and flat.

"You little...," reaching and grabbing for me, "I'm your mother! Don't think you can't get your little ass beat!"

I rolled my eyes, dismissing her with a wave. "Yeah, okay."

Grandma Louise interrupted; her voice was sharp.

"Pam, it's time for you to go. No need in getting these girls riled up."

She held the door open. Pam just stared at us; her eyes softened as they landed on Lydia. Lydia gripped my hand tighter as she remained silent.

I held onto Lydia's small hand. She was only four. She was still a baby in a lot of ways.

"Let's watch TV. What do you wanna watch?" I said, starting towards the back room before I glanced back at Pam, smirking.

"Cartoons," her little voice responded.

"Of course," I said, kissing her cheek. We continued walking into Grandma Louise's bedroom, and I turned on the television. The two of us stretched out across the bed on our elbows, nestled into over-sized pillows. I clicked through channels until I landed on Disney.

I watched my sister giggle at scenes from *The Loud House*; her small body quaked with laughter. Her laughter was both comforting and painful. I was furious at Pam for disappearing again.

The truth felt like a punch to my chest: *She doesn't love us.*

"We must not be good kids for a mother not to love us," I thought, swallowing the lump rising in my throat.

I sat up slowly, resting on my elbows as I faced my sister.

"Lyd," I called out softly, "we're not calling her Mommy anymore, okay?"

Lydia blinked several times.

"Why not?"

"Because she's not a mommy to us, is she?"

Lydia shrugged, her eyes dropping low.

"Then... what do we call her?"

I painfully stared off, blinking fast to keep my tears at bay, forcing another smile.

"Pam."

There was a slight pause.

"Mommies love their babies, right?"

"I guess," Lydia muttered, her smile slipping away.

We held hands and let the cartoons fill the room until we both drifted off to sleep.

* * *

Now, years later, I pressed the phone to my ear, my heart feeling heavy.

"We should've done more," Lydia said quietly; her voice was full of guilt.

"We did what we could, Lydia. She chose that life. We were just kids. We couldn't have saved her," I replied, shaking my head. "You know how she was. She didn't want help. She just... wanted to escape."

Pam's addiction had hung over our lives like a storm cloud. I lost count of all the nights I stayed up waiting for Pam to come home, or the times I'd found her passed out, unconscious.

Lydia let out a shaky breath. "I know. It just... it still hurts. Sometimes I wonder if she ever thinks about us."

I felt my tears burn my eyes. I had asked myself the same question more times than I could count. But there were no answers—just that hollow space where the thoughts of Pam used to be.

"I wish things were different," I said, swiping away tears. "We can't change the past. We have to keep moving forward."

After a long pause, Lydia asked the question that still haunted them both.

"Do you think she'll ever come back?"

I closed my eyes, allowing the silence to stretch between us. I wanted to offer comfort, wanted to pretend things would be okay. But the truth sat heavy in my chest.

"I don't know," I said quietly. "But I can't keep holding on to that hope, Lyd. It's breaking me."

"Yeah," Lydia murmured. "Me too."

We sat in that silence over the grief that had held us prisoners for so many years. Now, we were bound by shared grief and sad memories. And yet, in that stillness, something shifted. I felt the burden ease, just a little. The distance between us didn't feel so impossible anymore.

"I'm glad you called, Sis," Lydia said after a few minutes. "I've missed you."

"I've missed you too," I whispered, my chest tight. "Maybe we can talk more. I think we need that."

"Yeah," Lydia said. "I'd like that."

32

TURN AROUND

The trap spot sat on an L-shaped road littered with abandoned houses and half-collapsed buildings that looked like they should've been torn down years ago. Everyone in the city knew the place—called it Skid Row.

One of the local fiends earned the nickname "Skid" and claimed a crumbling three-story building as her own. She'd barricaded every door and window with barbed wire, warding off other squatters like it was her personal fortress.

A sleek black Mercedes-Benz eased around the corner, catching Skid's eye. Her head jerked toward the street, then back to the car.

"Wha—what's happening, Ace?" she asked, her voice jittery, calling me by the nickname she had given me a couple years back. Said I was her "Ace" because I was the only one who checked on her.

I leaned out the window, a crisp hundred-dollar bill pinched between my fingers. "You been alright, Skid? Take this. Do something good with it."

Skid took the bill carefully, scanning the empty block to make sure no one saw the exchange.

"I've been alright, Ace. Thank you. You know you don't have to do this."

Looking at her, I couldn't help but wonder who she used to be before the streets took a hold of her. She had been beautiful once. Not like the other fiends. Skid still had pride, even now. She held onto the kind of dignity most addicts lose early on.

I asked her the same question I always did. "Skid, I'm still trying to figure out how you ended up out here. What happened?"

She looked at me dead in my eyes, her expression lined with years and edged in pain. "Ace, we all got our own battles. You deal with yours your way, I deal with mine my way," she said, her jaw moving, chewing on nothing.

I nodded. "Alright, Skid. I got you. Just make sure you use that money for what you need. I'll be back around soon."

She gave a slow nod, bobbing her head like a beat was playing only she could hear. "Yeah, alright."

"Stay sharp, Sis," I said as the Benz rolled forward. "If you need anything, you know how to reach me."

And with that, I pulled away, the cracked pavement of Skid Row shrinking in the rearview mirror.

Latoya:

I stepped out of Bunkey's Market, plastic bag swinging lightly at my side. I glanced to my left and spotted a car idling at the curb.

A black Mercedes idled at the curb. Through the half-lowered driver's window, I caught a glimpse of the man behind the wheel. My stomach tightened.

"Is that Mario?" I whispered under my breath. But it wasn't just him; someone else was with him.

A tall young woman with long legs stepped out of the passenger side. She didn't look back, just started walking, heels clicking against the cracked pavement.

My chest tightened. Who is she? Without thinking, I followed her.

Block after block, the woman didn't slow down. I stayed far enough back not to be noticed, my heart hammering harder with each step. Finally, the woman slipped into a restaurant, the door swinging closed behind her.

I hesitated, then pushed inside.

The moment my feet crossed the threshold, cold steel greeted me. A chrome-plated nine-millimeter pointed straight at my face.

"Who are you, and why are you following me?" the woman demanded.

My throat went dry. "I—I saw you with my boyfriend."

"Your boyfriend?"

"Mario," I whispered.

The woman's eyes flickered, almost amused before she exhaled sharply. "Never heard of him."

"You were just in his car!"

The woman tilted her head. Her expression was unreadable. A small tattoo placed on her wrist. It was a coiled snake that slightly peeked out as she adjusted her grip on the gun. "Listen. You need to think twice before following strangers. Turn around."

My voice trembled. "Why? What are you going to do to me?"

The woman steadied the barrel, pressing the weapon closer to my forehead.

"Turn around—or black is the last thing you'll see."

My hands shaking, I obeyed her instructions. Behind me, the restaurant door opened, then shut. When I looked back, the woman was gone.

My knees buckled, and I sank into the nearest empty chair. My breath was ragged.

A seating attendant rushed over. "Ma'am? Are you alright?"

I forced myself upright. "I'm fine. I just—just need a minute." Without another word, I stood to my feet and hurriedly rushed out.

Shaken, I dialed Mario.

"Hey, baby!" Mario answered.

"Mario!" My voice cracked, frantic.

"Baby, what's wrong?"

"I need you to pick me up, and hurry!" I sobbed.

I gave him the name of the restaurant. Silence filled the line, then his voice boomed.

"Baby, I'm on my way! Walk down to The Bistro and I'll be there in less than five!"

My pulse spiked. "I just left Bistro's before walking here! Mario, what's going on?"

"I'll tell you everything when I get there. Just let the hostess know I have a table waiting for you. Don't say anything else."

Before I could press him for more details, the line went dead.

Minutes later, Mario was tearing down the street, jaw locked, his chest tight. His phone was already in his hand.

"Money," he barked the second Robert picked up, "we got a problem. Something just went down with Latoya! I need Mookie to get on those cameras at Bistro's. Check out the block from an hour ago."

"Cool! I'll meet you at the restaurant," Robert said.

When Mario reached the restaurant, he found me pacing in the VIP lounge, my face streaked with tears, and my hands trembling. The second I saw him, I collapsed into his arms, sobbing.

"Baby," he whispered, holding me close. "You're safe. I'm here."

He led me out the back door, settling me gently in the passenger seat. My eyes glistened with new tears as I turned to face him.

"Mario, what's going on?"

He brushed a kiss against my lips. "Let's get you home."

But as he pulled onto the road, his mind was already racing. Snake tattoo. Weapons being drawn. Whoever she was, she sent a message.

33

———

THE MAN WHO WASN'T DEAD

I sat behind my desk, finishing up with a few last-minute changes, when someone tapped twice on the door.

"Yeah?" I called out.

"Hey, Money, I got the drop on that dude that was stirring up trouble at the dungeon," Rosco said.

My eyes snapped toward Rosco. "Word? What you got?"

Rosco pulled a photo from his jacket and handed it to me. Before accepting the picture, I clapped my hands together and brushed the imaginary dust from my palms. The color drained from my face. I pinched the bridge of my nose, lowering into my chair as if the weight of the man in the photo hit me like a blow to my chest. The man was dressed in an expensive, dark, tailored suit.

"Money, you good? Boss, you good?" Rosco asked.

"Rosco, send someone to pick up Stoney and grab Mookie. Have them meet me in an hour."

One hour later, Mookie and Mario were standing in the penthouse.

"What's this about?" Mookie muttered.

Mario remained silent, deep in thought.

Mookie peered at Rosco. "Money didn't mention what he wanted?"

"Nah, he just told me to have you guys meet him here in an hour," Rosco said.

The double doors opened, and their attention shifted toward the entrance. Robert calmly walked inside.

"What's up, Money?" Mookie asked.

I rubbed my hand down my goatee. "I had Rosco check out that distraction down at the dungeon. The information he shared with me..." My voice trailed off, my words failing me.

Mookie and Mario watched me intently as I struggled to find the words. Mario walked over to me, placing his hand on my shoulder.

"You good? What happened?"

I shook my head. "Let me show you what I'm finding so hard to say."

I stepped out—and returned with a man no one expected to see.

Mario froze, his knees weakened. Mookie's hand shot to his mouth.

"Oh my god! I—I thought you were—!"

"Damn!" Mario whispered, finally finding his voice.

Marcellus, whom we affectionately called Manny, stood in the door-way, alive. His brothers rushed him, arms locking tight around his shoulders. Celebrating what they thought would never happen—finding the only family Mario had left.

After Mario told Manny what he had learned through Mr. Rufus, Manny shared the night someone tried to kill him four years ago. The attack left him bleeding, broken, and alone behind the club, where he thought no one would find him. Carmen, who had just left the

Dungeon with her friend Tammy, was heading to her car when she heard a low, desperate moan coming from the alley. Instinctively, she stopped in her tracks, telling her friend to go ahead and head home, saying there was something she needed to take care of, because she didn't want her to see him.

Once her friend made it safely to her car, Carmen came back to check on him, quickly noticing he was hurt in two places. He was shot once in the shoulder and once in the back. Manny told how he pleaded with her not to bring the police into it but asked her to help him get back on his feet. The bounty on his head and the threat on his life forced them to go into hiding in an abandoned apartment building unknowingly owned by the trio.

When Robert started making regular check-ins on the apartment building was when he first crossed paths with Carmen. Carmen was trying to keep strangers at a distance, telling him everyone called her "Skid." She pretended to be a struggling drug addict when she realized that Robert never judged her but instead offered her kindness. Because of his generosity, they were able to make ends meet while Manny recovered.

Manny went on to explain that during the time he and Carmen spent together, their bond grew stronger. Facing hardship side by side is when their relationship deepened. It was built on trust and loyalty. Eventually, those feelings grew into love. Once he was back on his feet, he and Carmen got married.

Someone was trying to take out his whole family. Mario was more determined than he had ever been to get his revenge.

34

___

DAMAGE THAT LINGERS

I paced the office floor during my session, my steps muffled by the carpet. I stared out the bay window, tears stinging my eyes.

"I find it strange," I whispered, "how a mother can't see the damage she caused her children. She called it a joke—I call it cruel. Twisted. 'I found you! You were left behind in a shopping cart!'" A bitter laugh escaped, but it faded quickly. I swiped at a tear sliding down my cheek. "For as long as I can remember, I have felt like I didn't belong."

Dr. Mendez scribbled a few notes on her pad. "Sounds like there's a lot there. A lot of family history, a lot you haven't shared with him yet. How does it feel, keeping that part of your life closed off?"

I shifted in my seat, the question settling heavily in my chest. I took a deep breath. "I don't know," I admitted. "I think... part of me is afraid that if I tell him everything, he won't see me the same. That it might change how he feels about me."

I looked up, meeting Dr. Mendez's calm, steady gaze.

"It sounds like you're protecting him from your past," she said gently. "What do you think you're protecting him from?"

My voice, when it came, was barely above a whisper.

"I guess... it's like a piece of me is still stuck in that horrible space. I don't even fully understand it myself—how do I explain that to someone else?"

"It's okay not to have all the answers right now. You're allowed to move through this at your own pace. When you're ready, we'll explore it together."

She set her pen down and offered a soft, reassuring smile.

Dr. Mendez suggested I find the loophole that left me feeling unworthy of love, starting from the last place I felt loved. That day Pam fled from the family reunion, Grandma Louise never mentioned the note Pam left behind. A few days later, I had built up the courage to rummage through Grandma Louise's documents when I stumbled across a letter Pam wrote to her. "Mama, I just left my son, your first grandchild, in a hospital. Mama, my heart is crushed, and I pray no other woman has to feel this pain. I know you hate me for sending Beau to prison, but what about me? What about me, Mama?"

I hadn't realized the tears had covered my face until a single drop fell onto the letter. What happened to Pam? What happened between her and Uncle Beau? I vaguely remembered my uncle and had never heard of an issue between them. I had a burst of urgency to find out. I rummaged through more papers until I found a stack of letters Pam had written to Beau. All the letters were returned unopened. Placing the letters in order by date, I opened the first envelope. "Beau, I hope this letter finds you swimming in hell!" read the first paragraph. I gasped as I read the second: "Your son was born at St. Barnabas Hospital in the Bronx, and he looks just like you! All because of you, his fate is sealed—never getting the chance to know me! I hate you!" Mario rushed to hold me as my body shook ferociously.

"Baby, what's wrong?" Concern was etched on his face.

I had put the pieces together. Beau was locked up for four years; I was born a year later! I rushed to the bathroom, unable to hold the contents of my stomach.

"No!" I screeched. "No!" I sobbed into my hands.

"Baby!" Mario whispered. "I'm here!" He assured me, rocking me as I cried in his arms.

Mario allowed me to stay in bed as long as I needed to—carrying me to the bathtub, bathing me when I didn't have enough in me to bathe myself, feeding me when I couldn't eat a single morsel. My strength had left me, depression standing in its place. Dr. Mendez prescribed something for my depression and video-called me regularly to make sure I didn't do anything to harm myself. Mario notified Lydia, informing her of my situation, giving her bits and pieces of my diagnosis. Lydia made sure to continually call to check on me as well.

A few weeks later, along with Mario, I secretly submitted a DNA test using the DNA taken on file from Beau when he went to prison. During the time it would take to receive the results, I busied myself journaling. I read and reread all of the short notes Pam had left for me during her addiction. She loved us. She said her children were her best creation—that we were the only things in her life that she had ever done right. I held the notes to my chest as I allowed myself to cry for the little girl who felt so unseen. Her innocence lost forever. Tears for Pam, the mother who tried to keep herself clean for her children but failed each time.

Two months later, my hands shook as I held the paternity results that arrived in the mail. As promised, Mario was right by my side. I slowly ripped the envelope, opening then unfolding the paper. Falling to the ground in disbelief—Beau was my father too.

A few years after he was released from prison, Beau was shot and killed during a dice game, accused of cheating. No one came forward to claim his body, so the state cremated him free of cost. There was no burial, no family, no loved one to send him off. No one except Jayden Michael Beaumont.

35

THIS IS YOUR LIFE

A few nights earlier, the plan Mario carved out was simple: Beans would sneak into New York's quarters and swap his live rounds for blanks. Moving with precision, Beans quietly entered the home of New York and replaced the magazine in the firearm, just as he returned the weapon beneath the mattress.

There was no time to spare to double-check his work.

He slipped silently through the adjoining bathroom and shut the door behind him. A woman's voice called out, "Who's there?"

Thinking fast, Beans flushed the toilet and opened the bathroom door. He staggered as if he were drunk. "Hey," he smiled.

The woman returned the smile. "No one's supposed to be in this section of the quarters."

"I'm sorry, I thought this is where he told me to go."

"No, I'm sorry—please follow me."

As she escorted him toward the guest area—

"Thank you."

"Of course."

* * *

"What are we waiting around for?" Beans asked, passing the blunt to New York.

"I'm waiting for the green light from Sarge," New York responded, taking the blunt between his pointer finger and thumb before taking it to his lips. He took a long pull when his phone chirped.

"Here we go!" New York said, passing the blunt back to Beans, then hurrying off to call back the number.

Beans eyed him as he returned excitedly, wearing a huge grin.

"It's party time!" he said as he clapped his hands.

"So, that was Sarge?" Beans asked suspiciously, staring straight ahead with a toothpick dangling from the corner of his lips.

Still grinning, "Yep!" he said, snatching his jacket from the chair.

As they arrived at the warehouse, it sounded like a war zone. Gunfire could be heard coming from inside.

"Where's backup?" Beans asked as they exited the vehicle, crouching low.

New York crept to the back where Beans was crouched.

"They're en route! Let's go ahead and move in... slowly!" he whispered.

Beans removed the toothpick from his mouth and tossed it to the ground.

"Alright, let's do this!" Beans said.

New York knitted his brows, twisting his lips into a scowl.

"Why you sound like you're mad about it! This is a good call! Let's get these niggas! Look, if you don't want to go inside, I get it. Just keep watch from here," New York muttered.

"Nah, I'm good! Let's get in there—the party has already started!" Beans said with a strained chuckle.

Making their way inside the warehouse, New York gave the separation signal, waving two fingers apart. New York went left and Beans went right. New York moved through the darkness, spotting Zander. Their eyes locked; a nod was exchanged. That was all he needed to execute everyone in the building. Moving throughout the building, he crouched low, only standing to fire off shots, until his laser landed on Beans.

"I'm getting you next, nigga!" he mouthed.

"Nefertiti," Beans whispered into the radio. Feeling eyes burning into him, he spun around, finding himself face to face with New York. New York wore a menacing grin as he pointed an unfamiliar weapon at him.

"What the fuck are you doing?" Beans asked, his eyes narrowing.

"Pop! Pop! Pop!" Shots blasted, slamming Beans backward. Pain exploded throughout his chest as he hit the ground, gasping for air.

New York's grin widened as he vanished into the smoke, leaving Beans on the cold floor, blood pouring out of his ears.

What Beans hadn't counted on was the live round left in the chamber during the switch. His ribs screamed; his lungs fought for air.

36

ANSWER TO ME

Zander tore through the streets, darting between cars and whipping up and down narrow side streets. Adrenaline pumping through his veins like fire. He snatched his phone, thumb dialing furiously.

"Speak!" Base's voice thundered.

"Aye, nigga, grab the others and listen closely—do exactly what I'm getting ready to say. Don't fuck this up!" Zander barked.

"Got it!" Base snapped back.

Hours later, Base and the crew stood outside the warehouse. Mario sat bound to a steel chair. His nose had been broken, his left eye was swollen shut, and his split lip had begun to swell.

The warehouse doors swung wide, slamming against the walls with a deafening bang.

His right eye locked in on a shadow that hurtled inside, hitting the floor. It was Latoya. Her eyes were wide with fear. When she noticed Mario, she took in deep breaths to steady herself—something she did as a child when she knew something bad was going to happen.

Mario feverishly pressed against the restraints.

"Did you fucking touch her?" he roared through bloody, gritted teeth.

"Easy, nigga!" Base sneered, ready to wreak havoc on him the same as he had with Latoya.

"If you lay a finger on her, I swear you won't just die—you'll die slow and miserable," Mario growled, never breaking eye contact with Base.

Powder cackled. "Nigga, how you gone do that?" he taunted.

Base raised his gun to Latoya's head. "Yeah, chill out, bruh, before I bless this bitch."

Mario thrashed in his chair as the blood trickled down his face. On the inside, his whole body trembled with fury—because he knew once he was set free from the ties, that whole crew would die.

The men stood unfazed and relaxed, laying their weapons casually along the countertop. Latoya didn't flinch as Powder and Base circled her, ripping her clothes from her body.

Zander stood back, eyeing Mario, feeding off his pain.

Base laughed boldly.

"I hear you stripper hoes like it when it rain!" He unzipped his pants and began spraying her. The room erupted in laughter.

Suddenly, the warehouse doors exploded.

"I hear there's a party and no one invited me!" A laid-back voice drifted from the smoke. "That's rude." The mystery man taunted.

He strolled in, surrounded by armed bodyguards flanked with AKs on both sides.

One henchman attempted to lunge.

"Reach, motherfucker, and I'll shoot you so many times your mama will catch bullets!" Mookie growled, appearing in the doorway.

The men froze. Their guns were out of reach.

As chaos continued to erupt, a slender woman dressed in camouflage sprinted toward Latoya. "Come with me—now!"

When the woman reached for her, Latoya saw the coiled snake on her wrist and pulled back.

"You've got to come now!" she yelled in a whisper. Instantly snapping out of her daze, Latoya did what she was told without hesitation.

In minutes, Mario's crew surrounded Zander's men.

Zander fought against the ropes as he was hogtied and dragged to an awaiting SUV, guarded by Tony and Chico of the Cuban Cartel.

Hours later, Zander was awakened by sharp, stinging slaps across his face.

"Wakey-wakey, nigga!" someone taunted from the shadows, followed by another slap.

He groaned; blood was crusted over one eye. Still feeling disoriented, he slowly came into consciousness.

"Damn, Mook, I thought you killed this nigga," Robert roared.

As the shadows came into view, Zander's focus was becoming clearer.

"Wh—what's that? What's that in your hand?" he croaked.

The figure grinned. "This? This is your life."

He stepped aside.

Zander's breath caught in his throat.

Standing before him was Sake—his former Asian connect. Calm. Deadly. Revving a handheld saw.

"Zander," Sake hissed, his voice low and venomous. "You're a sewer rat who thought you could run my operation without me finding out. You betrayed your own family."

The saw roared louder.

"And now," Sake leaned closer, his voice remaining low, almost tender, "you answer to me."

A LIGHT AT THE END

The call Beans made was to the brothers. When he couldn't reach Mario, that sent up a red flag. That's when it clicked for the brothers: not only was Latoya missing, but Mario was missing too. Mario told Latoya the story of reconnecting with Manny and discovering the woman with the snake tattoo was Carmen, Manny's wife. He also told her about his discussion with Beans regarding Treavor "New York" Beaumont and how they discovered he was her brother—the one no one knew about.

Before Zander took his last breath, he revealed he had killed Mario's family to keep him from testifying. By some cruel twist of fate, tragedy had touched them all: Mookie lost his family in a car crash when a car driving the opposite way struck them head-on, killing them instantly. It was a wound that would never fully heal.

There was a light at the end of the tunnel. The bulletproof vest had saved Beans's life—he was critical but alive. He eventually made a full recovery and was honored by the department for exposing the corruption of his partner. Though still on the force, his bond with the brothers remained unshaken. Family wasn't always bound by blood.

Weeks later, Mario leaned back in his seat as he looked at each of his brothers, a grin plastered across his face.

"Hey," he said, raising his glass, "I asked Latoya to marry me, y'all."

The table erupted.

Manny shot to his feet, clapping him on the back. "Congratulations, Bruh!"

"My man!" Mookie hollered.

Robert lifted his glass. "To you, Bruh!"

Ant arched his brow. "So, it's official? You're going to be cuffed for life now!"

The room filled with laughter. That kind of happiness you can't buy.

* * *

Later that evening, Mario sat in his parents' living room, nervous but excited at the same time.

"I proposed to Latoya," he said quietly.

His mother gasped, a hand flying to her chest, tears dancing in her eyes.

"Oh, baby, I don't even know what to say," she whispered. "She's a beautiful girl. You two are... you just fit."

His father rumbled with approval, voice thick with pride.

"You chose a good woman, son, and I'm proud of you."

Mario had no idea those words would mean so much to him—but they had. More than he'd ever admitted.

* * *

At the brothers' table, their vibe was everything.

"Look at Mario, all in love," Ant said, shaking his head, teasing him.

"He probably out here writing poems and shit," Mookie teased.

Laughter broke out again. Then Robert cleared his throat.

"Well... since we're sharing good news—I proposed to Chloe too."

The room exploded again.

"Yo, what?! Are you serious, yo?"

Mario embraced him in a tight, brotherly hug.

And then Mookie chimed in.

"Tiffany's pregnant! We just found out a couple of weeks ago. We wanted to wait for the right time to tell everyone."

A moment of shock, then silence—the room erupted again, louder this time, with chest bumps, cheers, and raised toasts.

Ant smirked, raising his glass, a playful smile tugging at his lips.

"Y'all out here settling down and shit. Me, I'm chilling. Living my best single life and killing it in the courtroom." He laughed.

Laughter echoed through the room.

We were men on our own paths. No matter what, we were brothers 'til the end.

The next day, Mario whispered into the phone, his voice trembling with emotion.

"Latoya, before we stand in front of everyone tomorrow, I just need you to know—my love for you is deeper than I ever thought was possible for a man like me. We've both been broken, but damaged doesn't mean worthless. We survived. And now we get to heal, together. I love you, Latoya Marie Beaumont. With everything in me. I feel blessed and honored that out of all the people in this world you chose to love me. I promise I'll never stop showing you how much I love you."

"I love you too," she sobbed quietly, because no one had ever loved her like this before.

The following evening, the sun poured golden light over Montego Bay. Waves crashed steadily against the shore as palm trees swayed in rhythm. Inside her glass-walled villa, Latoya stood before the mirror, robe loose, surrounded by Chloe, Trudy, and Mousey.

"I swear if my heart beats any faster, it's going to walk down the aisle without me," she laughed nervously.

"Girl, please," Trudy said, tugging rollers from her curls. "Mario's about to do that ugly cry when he sees you."

"Let him cry. That's the price you pay for marrying a baddie," Mousey teased, mimosa in hand.

"I'm excited. Like, butterflies and rollercoasters. I just... I still can't believe this is my life. We started off as a one-night stand. Now we're here, on an island. On a damn island!" Latoya said, pressing her hand to her chest.

"We're in Montego Bay, baby!" Trudy cheered.

"I just want everything to go perfect. Not fancy perfect, but us perfect," Latoya said nervously.

"And it already is. You're marrying your best friend. We're here, loving you through it," Chloe said, placing a reassuring hand on her shoulder.

Chatter filled the room, but when Trudy unzipped the garment bag, silence fell. The ivory gown glittered with subtle crystals, a sheer cape flowing like water.

"Okay," Latoya whispered, voice thick with tears. "Let's do this."

Outside, steel drums played as guests gathered on the sand. Mario stood beneath a floral arch of cascading ivory roses, crisp in his tux, eyes locked only on her. As Latoya walked the mirrored runway lined with orchids and candles, the world seemed to pause—waves hushed, the breeze stilled, and even time stood still.

The vows were real and honest, sparking laughter and tears from everyone there. The reception shimmered under cozy strings of light, with live jazz and clinking champagne glasses echoing into the night.

When Mario and Latoya shared their first dance, confetti drifted down upon them as gently as snow, and the cheers from their friends and family rolled in like waves.

It wasn't just a wedding. It was *the* wedding. The kind people would talk about for years, the kind where their love took center stage and everyone felt like they were a part of something special.

This night would always be remembered as the moment two hearts, two families, and a truly perfect love story lit up the coastline. They had made it through tough times, faced challenges, and carried scars. But together, they built something strong and lasting. Love, family, and forever.

ABOUT THE AUTHOR

Taye Knox is an avid reader and lifelong book lover from Dayton, Ohio. Her passion for stories began early and continues to influence her work today, inspiring her to write with curiosity, empathy, and a deep appreciation for the power of a good book. When she isn't immersed in a new read, Taye enjoys spending time with her family, exploring creative projects, and finding inspiration in the everyday moments that spark her imagination. Her writing reflects her love for storytelling and her belief that books have an incredible ability to bring people together.